"Your maidenly blush was quite something."

"It became fairly obvious you could understand my language," Lucien said. "I can understand why my calling you a termagant might cause the hackles to rise, but virgin?"

"It's not what you said," retorted Troy, "but the cat-and-mouse way you went about it."

"No insult was intended. I could have embarrassed you even more, had I chosen."

"I'm sure you could have, *monsieur.* Your imagination and expertise must be vast!" retaliated Troy scathingly.

"Ah, yes," Lucien said thoughtfully. "Now I recall another conversation you pretended not to understand. Something about a man being happy in your arms, was it not? And the delightful assertion that my bed would not be cold with you in it."

"I'd sooner sleep in the fields," Troy observed icily.

JACQUELINE GILBERT
is also the author of this

Harlequin Presents

160—DEAR VILLAIN

and these

Harlequin Romances

2102—EVERY WISE MAN
2214—COUNTRY COUSIN
2308—SCORPIO SUMMER
2492—THE TRODDEN PATHS

JACQUELINE GILBERT

a house called bellevigne

Harlequin Books

TORONTO • NEW YORK • LOS ANGELES • LONDON
AMSTERDAM • PARIS • SYDNEY • HAMBURG
STOCKHOLM • ATHENS • TOKYO • MILAN

For my husband

John

Harlequin Presents first edition June 1983
ISBN 0-373-10600-9

Original hardcover edition published in 1982
by Mills & Boon Limited

Printed in U.S.A.

CHAPTER ONE

'CHIN a little higher, Troy. Fiona, turn your shoulders more this way. That's it! Fine. Now, give me your haughty look, girls.'

Troy Maitland complied with Hal's drawled request, arching her finely shaped brows and pouting her mouth just a fraction. Haughty look, sultry look, outdoor-girl look were all within her range of expressions, and yet her reaction on seeing the finished product in the glossy pages of *Vogue* or *Harpers & Queen* was always the same, one of dissociation.

She would remember the day the photograph was taken. In this case the Hal Lindsey team had taken over the Cour du Cheval-Blanc at the Royal Palace, Fontainebleau, France, eight-fifteen on a May morning, before the Palace and gardens were opened to the public. Yes, the day would be remembered, and possibly she would recall her thoughts at the particular moment when her image was captured in a split second click of the camera. But the striking-looking girl so smartly dressed in a heather-coloured hand-woven woollen suit would not be the real Troy Maitland.

This shiny illusion was Victoria Maitland, a Hal Lindsey discovery, whose face and form were the perfect foil for promoting a new shampoo or perfume, or gracing the lines of a Jean Muir or Laura Ashley, a Mantana or Guy Laroche. The Victoria Maitland face was oval, with delicate skin tones, beautiful cheekbones, a straight nose and a pair of large brown eyes thickly lashed. A small, shapely mouth curved into a smile that could be cheeky or seductive, showing nice even teeth, and disguising a chin that, in repose, had an air of determination about it. Rich red hair sprang into natural waves and kiss-curls and fell in magnificent abundance to her shoulders. Tall, slim and long-legged, with natural poise and grace of movement—all this culminated in a certain indefinable 'something' that caught the eye and leaped out from the glossy page. This, then, was Victoria Maitland.

Troy Maitland was someone else altogether. The basic ingredients were the same, of course, but Troy Maitland's hair was pulled back and ruthlessly secured out of the way. She wore old and comfortable sweaters and jeans which were covered by an all-enveloping smock. The lavishly oiled and manicured hands would be plunged in wet, pliable clay, sensitively moulding to shape an unformed mass which would eventually emerge into a 'Troy' sculpture. Over the years, one or two of these had found their way in to a modest corner of a few reputable art galleries and thence into the home of some discerning art collector.

Hal Lindsey knew of the spare room converted into a studio, but persisted in burying his head in the sand regarding its importance, having never really believed that the glamorous world he had opened up to Troy was merely a stopgap, a means to an end.

Troy knew different. She had come out of college with a good degree and the determination to specialise in sculpture. She knew that progress would be slow, that until she made her name and earned a reputation she would have to get a job to support herself. She obtained one in the display department of an advertising agency and there met Hal Lindsey. He was one of the up-and-coming young men in the world of photography, and after persistent badgering, Troy sat for him.

Some days later a packet slipped through the letterbox and Troy stared for a long while at the glossy prints, the outcome of that sitting. She felt the first twinges of unreality as her face stared back at her.

Three years later her face and figure were still earning her the rent on the small terraced house in Bow that she shared with Fiona, and someone with less determination would have been seduced by the glamorous image she portrayed. Those few 'Troy' sales helped, together with the interest of Sir John Daviot, a distinguished sculptor, who hand-picked his pupils; only favouring those with promise.

According to Sir John, Troy had now reached the stage when her work needed total commitment and not half-measures. He suggested she enter for a yearly competition sponsored by a well-known art gallery in conjunction with a national newspaper. This meant giving up her job and concentrating on her art.

Troy valued his advice and while deliberating on it something happened that took control of her destiny. Her grandmother died. She was eighty-five and Troy's only living relative with whom she was close.

Her grandmother's death was a great loss to Troy and she left an intriguing inheritance behind, an unknown house in France. A house called Bellevigne.

With a five-day assignment in Paris already booked, Troy decided it would be her last. She would then take a much-needed holiday and search for this house at the same time.

So here she was, sixty-eight kilomètres south-east of Paris, on the last day of that assignment, and already beginning to feel excitement growing for the mystery that lay ahead.

'Right, girls, you can relax for a minute.' Hal's voice brought her sharply back to earth. She watched him adjust the highly complex and expensive camera equipment set up in the courtyard below, and gave an inward sigh. Hal Lindsey, tall and thin, fair-haired and good-natured, dressed in jeans and sweat-shirt, had been a good friend over the past years. She knew he was disappointed in her decision to finish and knew also that he would have liked to have taken their friendship a step further, given the slightest bit of encouragement. This Troy could not do. Hal was a good friend, an excellent boss, but nothing more.

Fiona gave a delicate yawn and Troy raised her brows, saying:

'Come, come, Miss McKay, this will never do. Can I see the ravages of a late night? Against the rules, you know. Was it worth it?'

'No, it was not,' complained Fiona, shaking her dark, smoothly coiffured head. 'One should never look up old flames. Absence dulls the memory.'

Troy grinned and allowed her eyes to wander round the Royal Palace. There was a deep sense of history about the place which appealed to her, and standing as they were on the famous curved horseshoe staircase, a prominent feature of the courtyard, she could easily imagine a host of royal personages who must have walked these same stairs and trod the same paving stones. Louis XVI and Marie-Antoinette, Napoleon and Josephine . . . she could almost see them, so strong was the atmosphere.

She took a deep, satisfying breath, savouring the clear air and wondered what it was about France that appealed to her so. It was always the same, whenever she came, this instant feeling of well-being. She loved England, of course, but there was something about France that stirred her senses.

Hal had been prowling the courtyard, assessing angles, and now raced up the staircase.

'What a fantastic setting this is for a farewell scene.' The words broke involuntarily from Troy's lips but they made little impression. Fiona merely raised a sceptical brow and Hal tweaked Troy's skirt and twitched Fiona's lapel before running back down again to the camera. Everyone froze. The photograph was taken and Hal called: 'That's it . . . thank you, everyone,' and Troy and Fiona made their way to the caravan that doubled as wardrobe and changing room.

It was a relief to get out of next Spring's fashions and into their own cooler clothes, for the May day was wonderfully warm. Troy was ready first and she joined Hal, who was staring thoughtfully across the grounds to the surrounding forest.

'Are the clients going to be pleased?' she asked, and Hal replied:

'With luck. British Wool Travels Anywhere.' His voice parodied an advertising slogan. 'Even to Gay Paree with the promise of a handsome, passionate Frenchman lurking round every corner,' he added dryly.

'I should be so lucky,' murmured Troy, lifting her face to the sun.

'Was that your own farewell scene you were speaking of, back there on the staircase?'

Troy pulled a face and shook her head. 'No . . . Napoleon Bonaparte's, you ignoramus! It so happens that he bade an emotional farewell to his Old Guard on that very staircase before being taken off to exile on

Elba. That's why it's sometimes called the Courtyard of Goodbyes.'

'How erudite of you, poppet,' drawled Hal. They began to walk back towards the caravan to meet Fiona, who had now emerged. 'One more session in the Bois de Boulogne and then we're finished,' he announced with satisfaction. 'You haven't forgotten the Descartes this evening?'

The two girls looked at him pityingly. Fiona spoke for them both.

'Hardly, Hal dear, when we've brought over new dresses especially for such an occasion. Who are these Descartes, anyway?'

'I know their son,' replied Hal, ushering the girls into his car and signalling to his assistant that the caravan was to go first. Climbing behind the wheel, he went on: 'They're bankers. Remember the Scarlet Pimpernel? Well, the Descartes would have needed his help to escape Madame Guillotine!' He engaged gear. 'I trust you're duly impressed?'

With the party going full swing that evening, Troy was even more impressed. The large room was beautifully decorated and furnished and the English trio were given a warm greeting by Armand and Jeannette Descartes. They were in their mid-fifties and spoke excellent English, much to Fiona's relief, although Troy would have liked the chance to air her French. The wine flowed copiously and when trays of food were brought round by the maids the choice was as varied as it was delicious. Someone refilled Troy's glass, murmuring: 'Charon, you understand . . . an excellent vintage,' and Troy nodded her agreement in what she hoped was a knowledgeable manner.

This same guest, as the evening progressed, seemed as intent on filling her glass as many times as his own. His name, he told Troy confidentially, was Georges, and he reminded her of an amiable teddy-bear. Recognising the signs of an amorous drunk in the making, she managed to lose him eventually by stepping out on to a balcony which she reached by a pair of long double windows, left slightly ajar.

She pulled the paisley shawl more securely round her shoulders and leaned forward against the rail, glad to leave the noise and smoke behind her, the night air, still retaining some warmth from the beautiful day, cooling her cheeks.

Perhaps Georges had done his work a little too well, she reflected wryly; the fresh air, on top of all that wine, was making her lightheaded. She grinned inanely to herself. What did it matter? Tonight was a half-way mark in her life. Behind her lay glamour and makebelieve, ahead—her face became serious for a moment—ahead lay the work she passionately wanted to do more than anything else in her life.

She gave a sigh and wished, a little bleakly, that her grandmother could have shared in this moment, and then gave herself a mental shake. Her thoughts, never far away from the subject, again returned to this house called Bellevigne .... Beautiful Vine. What would it be like? Was this the reason her grandmother had always encouraged her to continue with her French? A house! Troy felt mounting excitement which she had tried to bank down ever since the solicitor had told her about it. Just supposing it was possible to live in this house . . . convert it into a studio and work there!

A feeling of recklessness overwhelmed her and she laughed out loud and swung round, lifting her arms high and watching the silk fronds of the shawl swirl and billow through the air.

Come, this won't do, Troy told herself sternly but it was difficult to batten down the excitement. The lights of Paris twinkled tantalisingly before her as she gazed out into the darkness, the bridges over the Seine and the outline of the Eiffel Tower making a pretty pattern in the night sky.

She closed her eyes, listening to the muted sounds of the city. If she could choose, Paris would be the perfect place for a perfect love affair, she thought dreamily, and then laughed softly. No unique observation! And any place would be perfect, given the right man.

She opened her eyes and frowned thoughtfully. Why on earth was she thinking about love affairs right now? She leaned her chin contemplatively on her fist and reflected that at this moment in time there was no room in her life for a love affair. The only love affair for her was one with work.

Another, almost unnoticed sigh escaped her lips. Twenty-five and never been in love, never totally, blindly in love. She had had one or two minor skirmishes, but something had always happened to disillusion her. She expected too much, probably. Besides, they only seemed to want Victoria of the glossy print, not the real Troy, and were not prepared to share her with a lump of clay.

A reluctant laugh followed this observation. Really, this introspection would never do. She was in France, on the eve of an adventure, and indulging in dreams of romance was ridiculous and childish. Grandmother's death might have left her alone in the world, but that did not mean she had to run into the arms of the first man who held them open to her. That kind of comfort was a false comfort.

Interruption came abruptly on to the balcony as a

familiar figure staggered his way through the window, clutching a bottle to his chest. Troy swung round and watched his tottering progress and wondered with a spurt of amusement whether he would make it!

'*Ah! La petite anglaise! Enfin!*' Georges beamed at her, swaying slightly on the spot.

Troy hid a smile. *La petite anglaise* indeed! No one could call her five-feet-seven small, especially Georges, dumpling that he was!

Before she could make a reply Georges lurched himself amorously at her and the ensuing scramble had little dignity attached to it as Troy, trying to ward him off in the kindest manner, became showered with the wine from the now wildly erratic bottle.

The tussle ceased almost immediately. A figure came out of the darkness from the other end of the balcony, hidden until now by tall potted ferns. Before Georges knew what was happening he was lifted up and deposited out of harm's way. Surprise, and too much wine, made him stagger backwards before overbalancing completely into a tub of geraniums.

Once he had removed Georges, Troy's rescuer turned his attention to her. She was caught off balance and ended up clutched in a firm embrace, her cheek pressed against his shoulder, very conscious of a strong, wiry body and a pleasant after-shave.

How strange that only a few moments ago she had been reflecting on the comfort of being in a man's arms.

There was amusement in his voice as he murmured close to her ear:

'*Mademoiselle, permettez-moi, je vous en prie.*' She was set on her feet, his hands clasping her shoulders until she was steady, then taking the handkerchief from his top pocket, he went on in excellent English: 'Please, use this to mop up the wine. Georges is clumsy always.' Bright, humorous eyes stared at her intently. 'You are all right, *mademoiselle*?'

It was necessary to recover her dignity as well as her wits.

'Thank you, yes,' she said a trifle breathlessly, dabbing at the wet patch of wine, feeling his eyes still upon her.

'Good.' There was a pause and then he turned on his heel, remarking blandly: 'Georges! *Quelle bonne surprise!*'

A surprise, certainly, thought Troy wryly, whether a good one remained to be seen. Wine stain forgotten, she watched the ensuing encounter with interest. This man, whoever he was, had an air of authority about him and complete control of the situation, but she did not want Georges hurt; she had a soft spot for Georges. She need not have worried.

Georges stared blankly, his hand still clutching the bottle, and then he recognised the voice and in his own language exclaimed:

'Lucien! You are back in Paris!'

Had Lucien the slightest idea that Troy could understand French the conversation would not have taken the form that it did.

'Yes, Georges, I came especially for Jeannette and Armand's party.' Lucien bent down and heaved his friend to his feet, taking the bottle from him and placing it carefully on the nearby wrought-iron table. He then brushed him down solicitously in a way that made Troy want to giggle.

Georges waved a hand blearily somewhere in Troy's direction.

'Lucien, had I known you were with the so beautiful

anglaise I would never have interfered.' His voice was earnest and Lucien said soothingly:

'No, Georges, I know you wouldn't.'

'Couldn't compete with my old friend, Lucien, could I? But what a beauty! A man could be happy in those arms, eh, Lucien? Your bed will never be cold with her by your side. She has hot blood in her veins, I suspect, that one!' Georges embraced his friend emotionally. 'You deserve her, Lucien, my friend, you deserve her. How glad I am for you, old fellow . . . and she has kind eyes. Did you notice her kind eyes, Lucien?'

Lucien freed himself, urging Georges towards the windows. 'Yes, Georges,' he replied calmly, 'I noticed her eyes.'

Georges stopped in his tracks, hit by a sudden thought. 'Does Madeleine know about her, eh?' He began to chortle, touching the side of his nose knowingly. 'I won't tell her, Lucien, you can depend on me.' He smiled benignly. 'You sly fox, you!'

'Thank you, Georges, I am most obliged to you,' Lucien told him with remarkable composure, 'and now we will go this way . . .' and the rest of the sentence was lost as they entered the house, Lucien carefully closing the window behind him.

Troy began to giggle. Dear old Georges had her well and truly fixed with his friend. Hot blood in her veins indeed! But this Lucien, after the initial hassle, had been kind and gentle with Georges. She liked that in him. And he had not turned a hair at all the implications that she was sharing his bed. A tingling confusion swept over her as she remembered being held close to him, his hands resting on her bare shoulders. With a quick intake of breath she wrenched her thoughts away from the memory and her eyes caught sight of the tub of squashed geraniums. The giggle exploded into chuckles and she sank down on to a garden chair, visions of Georges with his legs waving in the air convulsing her into helpless silent laughter.

That was how Lucien found her on his return. Giving a smothered oath, he deposited the two glasses he was carrying and knelt by her chair, concern in his voice as he asked:

'Georges hurt you? Forgive me, I had no idea . . .'

Troy shook her head, pulling herself together. 'No, no, *monsieur*!' and hastily lifting a tear-streaked face from his handkerchief, went on brokenly: 'I . . . I'm so sorry,' and she pointed a trembling finger at the flattened flowers. 'P—poor Georges!' She began to laugh again and Lucien's troubled face, so close to hers, relaxed into a smile and his eyes crinkled attractively. Their eyes were level and Troy found that his were grey and quite startlingly intense. 'I'm sorry,' she said again, feebly, 'I think I've had too much wine.'

He rose and slapped halfheartedly at the knee of his trouser, then straightening, said: 'I'm glad you can see the funny side of the matter. You're very generous, *mademoiselle*, more generous than Georges deserves. I apologise on his behalf.'

Troy too had risen and in an effort to hide the peculiar fluttering of discomposure that this man seemed to be producing within her, replied quickly: 'No harm done,' she smiled,' 'apart from the flowers. I'm sure, when he's sober, that Georges is quite a sweetie.' She hesitated and said shyly: 'Thank you for your help.'

'It was nothing. I also apologise for not making my presence known to you before Georges's arrival, but the balcony seemed to be a large enough refuge for us both.'

There was a smile in his voice as if he were remembering her antics, then he indicated the glasses. 'I thought Georges's idea a sound one . . . but perhaps it would be dangerous to take more of this heady stuff?' and his brows rose questioningly.

Was there a challenge in his eyes? In the half-light Troy could not be sure. He wore no rings on his fingers and somehow she was sure that Madeleine, whoever she was, was not his wife.

Troy said lightly: 'Never let it be said that we English are scared of a bit of danger, *monsieur*,' and watched as he poured the wine into the glasses, taking one when it was offered. 'We can hardly toast danger, however, that might tempt providence, might it not?' and she lifted large innocent eyes to his, glass poised.

The grey eyes gleamed. 'How true. Shall we then drink to——' he stopped, thought a moment, and went on solemnly: 'chance encounters?' and without waiting for a reply raised his glass in salute.

Chance encounters was as good a toast as any, thought Troy, raising her own glass and taking a sip of the wine, for nothing could have been more chancy than this one. She studied him curiously and liked what she saw. Thick dark hair topped a long thin face, brow, cheekbones and jaw all prominent. Quirky brows were set above those startling grey eyes and a nose that was long and pointed. His mouth was wide and well-shaped with a slightly fuller lower lip, and a deep horizontal cleft redeemed an over-long chin. It was, she decided, a foxy face, sharp, bright and alert. Deep lines beneath eyes and either side of the mouth promised a sense of humour. He was a natty dresser too. A light-coloured pin-striped suit sat well on a slim, fit frame and a plain dark shirt with striped toning tie completed the sartorial ensemble. He was of medium height and looked to be in his thirties. Troy's eyes travelled back to his face, the artist in her responding to the interesting contours as her first instinctive thought was strengthened—that here was a face she could sculpt. Not the kind of thing one could say to a stranger.

She suddenly realised that the appraisal was mutual and, blushing, she turned to lean against the balcony rail. Would he make his excuses and leave? After a moment he joined her and together they looked out over the city.

The silence was not a particularly companionable one—how could it be, between strangers? Troy had always thought herself capable of making conversation, she had what was termed an easy, warm personality, and yet she was feeling oddly tongue-tied. It was unnerving. She was extremely aware of him, of his nearness, although his manner was certainly not obtrusive. In fact, it was almost detached. She was saved from making an inane remark by Lucien observing conversationally:

'Georges drinks to soften the fear of growing old and invariably makes a beeline for the most beautiful girl at the party.' His head turned and he smiled. 'I commend his choice this evening and ought to feel guilty that I'm standing in for him—but I'm not.'

How ridiculous to feel so pleased at the compliment, which had been voiced calmly and without the usual innuendoes. It was not true, of course, there was a bevy of beauty in the lighted room behind the closed windows, but she did feel that she was looking her best. She was wearing something of which she was particularly fond—wide-bottomed culottes. It was a striking outfit, the material fine and silky, in one of her favourite colours, a dark sea-green. The halter neckline enhanced the slope of her shoulders and the divided skirt emphasised her long legs and slim figure to flattering advantage.

'Georges means no harm,' Lucien continued. 'I've delivered him to his wife and she has taken him home.' He moved position, resting elbow and hip against the rail, his body turned towards Troy. 'It's a pity, is it not, when the passing years creep up unawares and the mirror becomes one's enemy? A pity, and quite futile.' For a moment there was austerity in the lines of his face and then, as swiftly, it was replaced by a humorous expression. The bright, alert eyes rested upon her. 'You have no need for worries as yet, *mademoiselle*, and as for me—*eh bien*! I never look in the mirror if it is to be avoided,' and his teeth gleamed in a slightly sardonic smile.

Oh, brother! thought Troy in comical dismay. He might not be handsome, but then handsome men had never attracted her, she reflected quickly, but he was mighty interesting! Never before had she met a man who physically attracted her so much, so soon . . . and that clever, whimsical face, she was sure, masked a keen, intelligent brain. She wanted him to go on talking, almost wanted to be disillusioned.

'Do you know the reason for this party, *monsieur*? I'm a last-minute guest and don't know my host and hostess.'

'Jeannette and Armand are celebrating their thirtieth wedding aniversary . . . *leurs noces de vermeil*. Do you not think they are to be commended?' A brow quirked.

'Ah . . . do I hear a touch of cynicism, *monsieur*?'

A gleam of humour flashed in his eyes. 'Possibly . . . although it was intended to be realism. I am only an onlooker, you understand, not a participant in the marriage stakes.' His flippant tone changed. 'Come, we will drink to Jeannette and Armand . . . may they continue to share happiness and good health together.' He drank and Troy followed suit. 'No need to drink to their wealth,' Lucien added slyly, 'for Armand is a wily banker. However, like Georges, he is a member of that dangerous age, the fifties, when we men try to turn the clock back!' He burst out into a laugh. 'You must forgive me if I am a little obsessed with passing time tonight, *mademoiselle*. You see, I am also having my own celebration, for I have reached the decidedly interesting age of thirty-four.'

'Today is your birthday?' asked Troy.

Lucien inclined his head. '*Oui, mon anniversaire*.' He shrugged eloquently. 'Perhaps I am not so different from Georges, after all. Maybe, at heart, we all want eternal youth and beauty.'

'You consider beauty to be an asset, *monsieur*?' Disappointment shot through her.

The amazing brows rose. '*Mais oui!* How can we possibly go through life without beauty?' His eyes narrowed, as if sensing he had failed her, and added dryly: 'But as no one person's idea of beauty is necessarily that of another's, life becomes delightfully unpredictable,' and he smiled lazily.

Troy found herself smiling back. She held out his handkerchief.

'Thank you for this. I would offer to wash it for you, but I'm moving on tomorrow.'

He put a hand to his forehead. 'What am I thinking of? Your culottes . . .'

'It's all right . . . the material is quite dry and my shawl took most of the deluge,' said Troy hastily, and looked vaguely round for the missing shawl.

'Nevertheless, the cleaning bill will be reimbursed.'

His voice became that of someone used to being obeyed.

'Very well,' assured Troy meekly, adding with a grin: 'It was too good a wine to spill.'

He shot her a look and then smiled his agreement. 'Here is my Paris address to which you will send the bill. You will humour me in this, *mademoiselle*?' and giving her a challenging look as if he intuitively knew that she intended taking the matter no further, he handed her a card which he had taken from his inner pocket, adding formally: 'Lucien Charon,' and paused, waiting.

'Troy Maitland,' supplied Troy, taking the card and slipping it into her bag.

'Troie?' He pronounced it in French, quizzically. 'Your name is an unusual one.'

'Troy is merely a childhood diminutive which stayed. My name is Victoria.'

'Victoire.' The name rolled over his tongue, giving it a new dimension. 'So, Victoire, you are *en vacances* in my country?'

'I'm just beginning my holiday, *monsieur*,' prevaricated Troy. Her personal history was far too involved to go into with someone she would never see again, and with the observation came the swift perception that she wished it could be otherwise.

His hand gestured to the city below. 'Paris in May is very beautiful.'

'I think Paris is beautiful any time,' confessed Troy, and received a slanting glance.

'Ah, we agree on one form of beauty, *mademoiselle*.'

She gave a soft laugh. 'So we do,' and went on a little diffidently: 'You speak excellent English, Monsieur Charon,' hoping that he would satisfy her curiosity.

He gave a deprecating shrug of his shoulders. 'I spent two years working in one of your large banking organisations. It is necessary to learn your language, Mademoiselle Maitland. The English, as a general rule, do not put themselves to the task of learning any tongue but their own and are most annoyed when they cannot be understood.' There was no force behind his words, the tone was lightly bantering.

It drew forth a reluctant laugh from Troy, who said ruefully: 'I'm afraid you're right.' She almost told him then that she was outside the general rule, that she had put herself willingly to the task. The desire to surprise him, to please him, rushed over her and her lips opened and closed, the words swallowed. Her fingers tightened on the glass in her hands, her thoughts in a jumbled whirl. This is ridiculous! she thought wildly. I hardly know the man—why should I want to please him? Confusion swept over her and she was desperately trying to nerve herself into making a casual exit when light spilled out from the room over them.

'Lucien? *Tu es là!*'

They turned as one at the exclamation and for a moment no one spoke and then Lucien replied quietly:

'Isabeau . . . *je viens tout de suite.*'

Isabeau, Troy could tell, was not altogether happy with this information. When she called she expected Lucien to come, not to have to wait, even for a few minutes. She gave Troy a sweeping glance before turning on her heel and walking back into the room. With the light behind her it had been impossible to see her features clearly, but Troy was left with the impression of a slim, petite woman with ash-blonde hair and a pleasing voice.

Troy glanced at Lucien Charon, but his face gave no clue to his feelings or thoughts. He made no attempt at an explanation. Isabeau's interruption might never have happened. She gave an involuntary shiver. Yes, he could be ruthless, this man, and Troy felt a momentary pang of pity for the unknown Isabeau. Lucien must have noticed the shiver, for he said:

'It is, perhaps, time we returned indoors. The night air is growing cooler and you will become chilled if you stay out here longer.' He looked round for her shawl and picked it up from where it lay on the chair. Taking the glass from her hand, he placed it, with his own, on the table and with a swirl, the shawl was draped round her shoulders and he stood for a moment looking down at her.

Time seemed to be suspended. Troy lifted her eyes to his and everything else—the noise of the city below, the subdued murmur of voices behind the lighted window, slightly open—everything faded into nothingness.

They were not touching. A few inches separated her from him, his hands still holding the ends of the shawl. If she made the least sign of resistance he would let her go, she knew this instinctively, but she was a willing prisoner. There was something about Lucien Charon that drew her from the first, an amazing leaping of the senses. It had thrown her off balance by the swiftness and the strength of his magnetism, and even now, part of her wanted to run.

As the blood rushed through her veins, pounding in her ears, sending her heart thumping madly, recklessness triumphed over caution, and she remained where she was, outwardly cool, inwardly a flutter of nerves.

Lucien gave a quick derisive smile, observing smoothly: 'Ah well, it is, after all, my birthday,' and pulling the ends of the shawl towards him he gathered her into his arms.

It was almost as if she knew what it would be like, his

bony sharp body against the softness and roundness of her own. As their lips met she closed her eyes, her body instant fire, his hands, moving beneath the silk shawl across her bare back, gentle, tentative.

At what point the kiss changed Troy was hardly aware. The delicate, almost teasing quality of his mouth upon hers was stilled in a split second of mutual astonishment and then his hands were no longer gentle and tentative, his lips no longer teasing.

And then she was free, cheeks flushed, eyes brightly shining, wide and startled, lips slightly parted, tremulous and glistening as she stared at him, dazed and breathless.

Lucien Charon stared back, intent grey eyes hidden by hooded lids as he stood, body tense and almost wary, and then he relaxed and the familiar whimsical expression flashed across his face. Eyes now brimming with laughter, he said:

'I refuse to apologise. Thank you, that was a delightful birthday present, Victoire.' He caught one of her hands in his own and raised it without affectation to his lips, his eyes still upon her. It trembled in his grasp.

Troy tried to collect her scattered wits and murmured feebly: 'Happy birthday, Lucien.'

What might have been said or done then was lost for ever as the window was pushed wider and a young voice burst out in French:

'Lucien? Are you there?'

Unhurriedly Lucien turned, releasing her hand which he had retained, saying calmly:

'Yes, Juliette, *mignonne*?'

The newcomer, who had now taken a couple of steps on to the balcony, eyes peering into the darkness, gave a sigh of relief.

'Lucien, they are about to cut the cake and make the toasts.'

'Thank you, Juliette, for warning me. I shall come immediately. Do not panic, little one.'

Juliette cast a slightly curious glance in Troy's direction, gave a shy smile before slipping back into the house.

Youth and beauty. The girl was young, not more than twenty, and very pretty. She seemed to make the five years dividing them much more, and Troy gave another shiver. Lucien was right—the years passed too quickly.

'Come, it is time we rejoined the party.' Lucien walked to the window and pulled it wider, letting out the sounds of laughter and talking, the light shining on his face, making him once more into a stranger. He gestured politely for her to pass before him. As she came level he said: '*Bonsoir*, Victoire.'

Her eyes flickered to his face, finding his expression difficult to interpret. She replied gravely:

'*Au revoir*, Lucien,' and brushing past, she walked into the party.

Hal was easy to find—tall and fair, he stood out in the crowd. Troy made her way to his side, suddenly glad to see him. He gave her a wide smile in greeting and put his arm round her shoulder, drawing her into the conversation.

After a few moments, almost against her will, Troy looked back towards the window. Lucien Charon was standing, his eyes upon her, face thoughtful. As contact between them was made Troy felt again the stirrings of something intangible inside her, a confused mixture of feelings, and then contact was broken as Juliette ran up, taking Lucien's arm possessively and laughing up into his face.

Lucien allowed himself to be drawn away, a smile on

his face, an arm draped carelessly round the young girl's shoulder.

Troy watched them go, the confusion of feelings resolving into two clear-cut ones. Disappointment and relief.

CHAPTER TWO

'HE looked,' observed Fiona decidedly, 'the type who gobbles up little girls like you for hors d'oeuvre.'

Troy laughed protestingly. 'Now, Fiona! Be fair, have I ever been gobbled up yet?'

'No, but that's the danger. One of these days you're going to let down that guard of yours and fall, hook, line and sinker. When that happens it had better be the right man.'

The waiter placed coffee and croissants before them and when he had gone, Troy said dryly: 'I don't think you need worry. A chance encounter in a foreign country, at a party given by strangers, is hardly likely to lead to my downfall. He was interesting, though.'

'Yes, he looked it,' drawled Fiona. 'Married?'

Troy poured the coffee and shook her head. Fiona bit into the croissant and deliberated.

'Pity he wasn't taller . . .'

Fiona tended to judge men from her own lofty height of five-nine. Troy said absently:

'Tall enough.' She passed over a cup of coffee. 'He could give you a couple of inches.'

'Sort of ugly-attractive,' went on Fiona. 'Occupation?'

'He spoke of banking.'

'When are you seeing him again?'

Troy gave a laconic: 'I'm not,' and Fiona stared at her.

'Honestly, Troy, I don't understand you,' she complained. 'You're damned attractive, intelligent, and yet . . . what did you talk about?'

'We discussed growing old,' Troy told her calmly, and Fiona looked aghast. Troy grinned. 'It was his birthday, his thirty-fourth, to be precise.'

'Mmm . . . and not married . . . and you talked about growing old!'

Troy laughed at the disgust in her friend's voice. 'He has depressing views on the subject of marriage, hence his bachelorhood. He likes women, only I got the impression we're a necessary evil.' She sipped her coffee thoughtfully. 'I'd have liked to have worked on his portrait, though.'

'Is that all he was to you?' demanded Fiona. 'A possible model? Troy, love, you're beginning to worry me. Didn't he stir *any* feelings other than professional ones, for God's sake?'

Troy raised her brows, eyes brimming with laughter. 'If you have to be so nosey, yes, he did . . . but it was probably because of his gorgeous French accent. His name, too, was rather attractive—Lucien Charon.'

Fiona said despairingly: 'Single, moneyed and attractive—why didn't you bring him to the point of exchanging telephone numbers, at least?'

'Because it looked to me as though he had enough woman trouble this side of the Channel without going across the water for more . . . and besides, I don't want to get involved. I've too much to do.' She ignored Fiona's grimace and added: 'Here comes Hal.'

Hal Lindsey sank into the empty chair at their table and groaned, lifting dark glasses for an instant, eyes painfully squinting, before dropping them back into place.

'Good morning, Hal,' soothed Troy. 'I'll order more coffee, you'll feel better when you've had at least two cups.'

'I doubt it.' Hal put a hand to his forehead. 'I should never drink wine, it always gives me a head the next day. How come you two look as fresh as daisies?' He watched gloomily while coffee was replaced and then asked Troy: 'Are you still determined to go off searching for this house?' and Fiona interjected with a positive: 'Of course she is.'

'I'm due a holiday and this seems a good time to take it, Hal. I've had the M.G. overhauled, I can speak the language and I'm curious,' Troy told him reasonably. Hal glared at the last croissant.

'Is that for ornament?'

Troy pushed the plate over to him. 'Be our guest,' she urged, hiding a smile. After a moment, she went on quietly: 'Don't think I'm attaching too much importance to this house, Bellevigne, but I am intrigued. It's caught my imagination . . .'

'What does it mean, Belveena?' asked Fiona curiously, and Troy smiled at her pronunciation, explaining:

'Beautiful vine. I expect all that area is vineyards and wine country.' She bit her lip thoughtfully. 'Of course, Grandmother was eighty-five and although remarkable for her age she did wander a bit towards the end. As she only ever spoke of France once, when I was in my teens and going on a school trip, I'm a little cautious about this inheritance of mine.'

'What did she tell you?' asked Hal, interested despite himself.

'I gather that when she was a young girl of about eighteen she came to France to do voluntary nursing during the first world war, it was called V.A.D., short for Voluntary Aid Detachment, if you remember. I can only think that her time over here then had something to do with the house, Bellevigne. I might be on a wild goose chase.'

'How can you be?' objected Fiona. 'Your solicitor says that the quarterly payments came from France.'

'Yes, they came from Bellevigne,' agreed Troy, 'but he knows as little about it as I do. He's merely the agent. I have the address of the legal firm in Paris and my solicitor has written to them about Grandmother and told them I'm her sole beneficiary.' She ran her fingers through her hair in frustration. 'You know what lawyers are like, slow as snails, so when this job came up, I thought . . .'

'. . . that you'd kill two birds with one stone,' finished Hal heavily. 'Where is this place?'

'Sève, a village on the banks of the River Loire, about a hundred kilometres south of Orleans,' replied Troy. She looked at her watch. 'You two had better move if you want to catch the ferry.' She pushed back her chair and stood up, looking fondly at her friends. 'I'll keep in touch,' she promised.

Troy stayed the first night in Orleans. She was in that curious state of wanting to reach Sève and yet feeling a reluctance to actually arrive there, in case disappointment awaited her. In any event, she told herself sensibly, she was on holiday, and Orleans was proving to be an interesting city, even apart from Joan of Arc. She visited the Musée des Beaux-Arts, the Cathédrale of Ste-Croix and the Hôtel Cabu to satisfy her artistic hunger, and the following morning spent some time wandering through street markets shopping for her bodily hunger. She purchased goat's cheese and pâté, a crusty baguette and fresh fruit, before setting off for Sève.

To leave Orleans it was necessary to cross the Loire, wide at this point, via the Pont George V, and with a spirit of adventure Troy headed the M.G. southwards. As the distinctively British open sports car sped along, its red paintwork gleaming in the sun, complementing Troy's red hair as it streamed out behind her, it attracted much attention. She found herself subjected to innumerable pap-paps from passing Renaults and Citroëns driven by grinning, appreciative Frenchmen. Amusing and flattering as this was, she was relieved when it was time to branch off from the International Highway on to one of the quieter side roads as she cut across country. In this calmer environment her thoughts drifted to Lucien Charon. It was possible now to smile about what had happened between them the previous evening and put it in its rightful perspective. She grimaced ruefully . . . too much wine on too empty a stomach, pre-holiday excitement and a madly attractive, intelligent Frenchman! She stood no chance!

Sève was reached without difficulty in time for mid-morning coffee. She loved it at first sight. Quaint and picturesque, it was little spoilt by tourism and still retained its old-world charm. Perched high on a hill above vine-covered slopes and surrounded by staggering views, Sève consisted of narrow, winding, climbing streets, tightly lined with old stone houses and shops.

Troy parked the car and wandered the streets, unconsciously seeking a house-name of Bellevigne. She was aware of curious glances from the inhabitants and was amused. Perhaps the people of Sève had never seen a jump-suit before? In pale yellow cotton, it was perfectly respectable, the front zip reaching from the mandarin collar, only her arms were bare, but it was a figure-conscious garment and did show off her lovely long-legged shape to advantage.

But Troy was used to stares and did not allow the

interest to disburb her. She came out on to a small square in the centre of which stood a monument naming the Sève men and women who had fought and died in two world wars, and she paused for a moment, saddened by the list of names. A notice, further on, attached to a small church, told her that Sève was a former Protestant stronghold and that the ruins of a round, fifteenth-century keep was all that remained of the old fortress of the Comtes de Sève. Troy now realised that Sève must have been a walled town and liked the idea of it perched high on its hill, warding off invaders . . . it appealed to her vivid imagination.

A pavement bar bordering the square beckoned invitingly, and here she was served an excellent cup of coffee, glad of the shade provided by the awning above, for the sun was now extremely hot. As she contentedly sipped the coffee, her eyes wandered round the square, taking in the typically French scene—the white stuccoed buildings, the tiny dormer windows, coloured shutters and windowboxes, the narrow cobbled streets leading off and the gay umbrellas of a rival bar.

The bar-keeper, when asked, directed her to a farmhouse, where it was possible to find inexpensive accommodation, and as she made her way back to the car Troy wondered how long it would be before the whole of Sève knew that an English girl had come to stay. The place had a feudal air about it and more than likely everyone knew everyone else's business!

She slowed the car to a stop before starting the descent down the hillside. It was a fantastic view—rows and rows of vines in regimented lines and in the distance, the glistening blue of the River Loire as it wound its way peacefully through the greenery, hidden now and then by a thickness of trees, appearing a little farther on, wide and sand-banked, separating round a willow island to disappear altogether behind the curve of a hill.

A pang of hunger reminded Troy that she wanted to get settled in somewhere before having her picnic lunch, so she started the M.G. and drove carefully down the hillside.

The bar-keeper had termed the farm as being '*ferme attachée au domaine*' which Troy took to mean being part of an estate, in England called the Home Farm. She followed the directions and swung the car through an open field gateway, checking the name 'Marin' on the top bar, before driving along a smooth, well-surfaced track. She pulled up before the final gate which led into a stone-paved farmyard.

The sprawling farmhouse was washed a pale pink, sporting spotless white shutters and a bright red door. Troy liked the look of the place and leaving the M.G., pushed open the gate. A dog came bounding round the corner of an outbuilding, barking, but it stopped when a dark-haired, middle-aged woman appeared at the porch and called to it sharply.

'Madame Marin?' asked Troy, and explained in her excellent French what she wanted and who had sent her.

Madame Marin nodded and replied: 'Ah, my husband's cousin, *mademoiselle*. Yes, we have a room to spare which might suit you. Perhaps you would care to look at it?' She turned and led the way into the farmhouse, which was spotlessly clean and shaded cool by the shutters. As they climbed the curving stair, Madame Marin asked over her shoulder: 'For how long would you need the room?'

Troy hesitated. 'I'm not sure, *madame*, but for one week at least. Would that be acceptable?'

'Surely. If you would come this way?' and Madame

stepped aside and ushered Troy into an attractive bedroom with a sloping roof and dormer windows. The floor was polished wood with scatter rugs, the bed covered with a patchwork counterpane and the furniture, sturdy and old, smelt of polish. From the window, Troy could glimpse the river, part of a wood bordering a strip of pasture and to the right, the lower slopes of the vineyard. She turned, smiling.

'This will do beautifully, *madame*, thank you.'

Terms were agreed, cases were unpacked and then Troy set off to find the river. Apple blossom in the orchards and hawthorn blossom in the hedges attracted her eye as she drove down the country lane. She gave a sigh of pleasure as she parked the M.G. on the grass verge near the entrance to a rough path through the trees. She lifted out the carrier bag which held her market shopping and set off down the path.

She took her time, for she was in no hurry. The wood was cool and speckled with sunlight, but it was soon apparent that she was not getting any nearer to the Loire. Coming to a clearing, she decided to be satisfied with that. It was a delightful spot and had the added attraction of a stream, which tumbled and fell over rocks, hurrying on its way to the big river.

Troy sat herself down on a mossy bank and ate her lunch. She finished off with a juicy nectarine and viewing her sticky hands went to wash them in the stream. It was very hot and the water looked inviting. She took off her sandals and rolled up the trousers of her jump-suit to her knees and stepped into the stream. The water was ice-cold and clear and also very rocky underfoot. Troy made her way gingerly up stream a few yards to a small waterfall.

It was an idyllic spot, and she held her hands beneath the cascading torrent, splashing her face and arms with the water, and only when her feet began to feel numb did she turn to make her way back. A movement on the bank caught her eye, making her stand still in the middle of the stream, her balance on the rocks precarious.

A dog was watching her from the bank. It was a breed she did not recognise, short-coated, grey-haired, with long legs and cropped ears, a short tail and a long bearded nose. Know the breed or not, the way its eyes were fixed upon her decided Troy to treat the animal with the deepest of suspicion.

She was not, in the normal way, afraid of dogs, but it now flashed through her mind, rather late, that she could be trespassing, in which case her predicament was very real. Before she could decide what to do, the undergrowth parted and out bounced another dog, twin to the first, who gave a short, deep bark before planting himself next to his brother.

Two pairs of eyes now stared across the water and suddenly the stream, the waterfall and the woods were no longer idyllic. Troy moved cautiously and heard a warning growl.

Damn and blast! she thought despairingly, and wondered what the trespassing laws in France were. A thin piercing whistle sounded through the trees and with one accord the dogs swung round and shot back through the undergrowth.

Seizing her chance, Troy began her hurried return, picking her way gingerly but with haste over the stones and rocks, arms outstretched for balance, wincing when the sharp edges cut into the soles of her feet.

The dogs' return pulled her up short and left her perched precariously on a particularly unsafe rock. When a man, carrying a sporting gun, followed in their tracks, amazement swept away the frustration and fear, leaving her wide-eyed in astonishmment.

'Good heavens! You!' she exclaimed, registering the ominous look of displeasure on Lucien Charon's face before she toppled, arms flailing wildly, into the stream. For a second the shock of the cold water took her breath away and then, as pain shot through her right thigh, a cry escaped her lips before being silenced by a clenched jaw.

She heard footsteps come splashing through the stream and she made an effort to struggle to her feet. Brown riding boots came into view and then she was hauled upright and swung up into his arms. Lucien Charon ploughed back through the stream and dumped her down, giving a stern: '*Couché*' to the dogs, friendly now and inquisitive.

Troy gritted her teeth, scowling with the pain, and clutched her thigh. She could still hardly believe that it was Lucien Charon who had amazingly appeared out of nowhere, and lifting her eyes, she said ungraciously:

'What are *you* doing here?' and Lucien replied grimly:

'I might, *mademoiselle*, ask the same of you.'

The colour flared to her cheeks beneath his sardonic look. 'You needn't think I followed you from Paris,' she told him shortly, and as she spoke she raised her palm and found it covered with blood. In some dismay she watched an ominous patch spreading brightly over the yellow cotton where the material had been pierced by the jagged rock.

Lucien muttered something under his breath and quickly knelt by her side, brows lowered. He took a swift glance at her face and said sharply:

'This is no time to faint!'

Troy bit her lip and ground out: 'I have no intention of fainting.'

'Good.' He placed his hand firmly in her groin, ignoring her wince of pain, and went on: 'I don't think it's too serious, but you must see a doctor. First we must try to stop the flow of blood.' He gave her jump-suit a sweeping look. 'Can you get that thing off?'

'Of course I can,' snapped Troy, 'but I'm not going to.'

'So you bleed to death through modesty? *Mon Dieu!* How can I deal with the wound if I cannot get at it? Surely bra and briefs can serve efficiently?'

'I am not wearing a bra, and I am not taking it off,' she said grimly.

'Bah! I see more bare flesh on our beaches each summer!' Lucien snarled and Troy muttered: 'Not mine, you don't,' and then he snapped: 'Press your hand here, exactly where my fingers are.'

Troy did as she was bidden and watched him seize the leg of the jump-suit between his hands and rip it open at the seam from ankle to thigh. He then proceeded to tear off a strip and while tightening this round the top of her leg, brusquely nodding to indicate she was to take away her hand, he asked shortly:

'What were you doing, anyway?'

Troy clenched her jaw, repulsed and yet fascinated by the jagged wound, wondering how such a silly accident could produce such drastic results. She looked at Lucien and blanched at the mess he was in and felt like weeping. His: 'Well?' made her start, and embarrassment and weakness made her lash out.

'Me? I was doing nothing, merely washing my hands. It was your wretched dogs who frightened the life out of me!'

'*Une absurdité* . . . they would not have hurt you.' Another strip was rendered, a handkerchief produced as a pad, and the strip used this time as a bandage. He shot her a quick look as a gasp of pain escaped her lips and frowned down as he worked.

'I'm very pleased to hear it,' observed Troy sarcastically, a silly wobble in her voice stirring her on indignantly: 'They look ferocious brutes and when I moved they growled. Was that an indication that they wouldn't hurt me?'

Lucien glanced again at her face and his reply was quite mild:

'They have been trained to guard only.'

'Perhaps you should hang a placard round their necks, *monsieur*, informing innocent bystanders of this fact,' muttered Troy, but her heart was no longer in it. She felt cold, uncomfortable and in pain. She leaned back against the tree and closed her eyes. She heard him move through the undergrowth, hiding the gun and the remains of her picnic, felt him slip on her sandals and then call: 'César . . . Satan!' to the dogs and his shadow fell across her.

'Put your arms round my neck.'

Her eyes opened. 'I can walk, thank you.'

'You will do as you are told, Mademoiselle Maitland,' came the voice of calm authority, and she was lifted into his arms and found it necessary to obey.

There was nothing dignified about the whole affair, she thought miserably, trying to ignore his face only a few inches away from her own. He obviously considered her to be a designing female and an idiot to boot.

She wanted to lay her head on his shoulder and have a good bawl, but pride forbade that. How overbearing he had been, and not one word of sympathy! So his sporting activities had been curtailed by a stupid English girl and he had taken a wetting—was that any reason to snap and snarl? Horrid man! How *dared* he think she had come chasing down here after him! Who did he think he was! These indignant observations did much to banish the momentary feeling of tears and her lashes lifted to find his eyes resting upon her.

Small drops of perspiration were beading on his forehead, although his breathing did not seem to be laboured. His gaze went back to the way ahead and as if reading her thoughts he said:

'You're not the lightweight you look, *mademoiselle*,' and giving a sardonic twist to his mouth, he added dryly: 'And I am no Hercules. Luckily, we have arrived.'

Indignation again stirred in Troy's breast and she thought bitterly of the romantic image that depicted Frenchmen paying flowery compliments. A number of sarcastic replies hovered on her lips but remained unuttered. Somehow, she knew that she would only come off the loser, and despite his claim to being no Hercules he had managed her well enough. She allowed herself to be placed along the back seat of an open jeep-type vehicle which was parked alongside the M.G. Giving her a shrewd look, Lucien tossed a sweater to her from the front seat and she struggled into it, pulling the ample folds down over her. She said stiffly:

'What about my car, Monsieur Charon?'

The two dogs jumped into the front and Lucien climbed behind the steering wheel, throwing over his shoulder:

'I'll get someone to fetch it later.'

With swift sureness he backed the jeep on to the road and began to drive back the way Troy had come earlier. She sat, clinging to the back seat, trying to come to terms with fate. This morning she had put all thoughts of Lucien Charon behind her, to be slotted into memory, a whimsical romanticism over which to smile a little. Now here he was, very much in the present, with nothing whimsical or romantic about him . . . arrogant, bossy and rude!

She lifted her face to the warm breeze, the awful feeling of faintness passing. The sweater was a comfort and the regular throbbing in her leg was bearable if she did not move it. She stared at the man behind the wheel. He was concentrating on the road ahead, hurrying, but taking no unnecessary risks, judging the bends to a nice degree as they wound their way up the hill to Sève.

Lucien slowed as he negotiated the narrow, climbing main street, nodding a greeting or lifting a hand briefly to shopkeepers standing talking in their doorways, or pedestrians pausing to watch them go by. Troy was again conscious of curious scrutiny as she sat, for all to see, along the back seat and smiled grimly to herself. Let him get out of this, she thought unfairly.

They swung round by the church and pulled to a halt. Troy had time to notice that the house was one of a row of old stone cottages, a brass plate by the door proclaiming: 'Marcel Dubois. Médecin.' before she was being carried down a dark, narrow passage.

Lucien shouted: 'Colette! *Une cliente pour le docteur! Faites vite!*' and nudging the door open with his foot he turned into the surgery. He had just placed her on the couch when a booming voice declared in French:

'What is all the noise? Ah, Lucien! An accident, eh?'

The newcomer gave Troy a shrewd glance, his eyes passing to her bound thigh. Moving to the wash-basin, he asked abruptly: 'What has happened?'

'She's English, a tourist, and has fallen on a rock. It looks nasty and there's been quite a blood loss,' offered Lucien as the doctor dried his hands and crossed to the couch. He undid the makeshift bandage and examined the wound.

'Hm . . . you did right to bring her.' He worked in silence for a moment, cleaning the wound, and then foraged in a nearby cupboard, and finding what he was looking for, returned, giving her another quick look before quipping: 'It would be a shame to mar such a fine pair of legs like these, eh, Lucien?'

Really, thought Troy resignedly, I shall have to let on soon that I can understand French!

Lucien drawled: 'You're an old reprobate, Marcel.'

'You think I'm too old to appreciate a good pair of legs, my boy?' and the doctor chuckled. Lucien grinned.

'Obviously not. Do you need me?'

'Of course I need you. Is it not Thursday, the day when Colette travels to Gien to see her sister? Hold this,' and he thrust a bowl into Lucien's hands and turned back to Troy, speaking to her in English.

'Now, young lady, I am going to give you a local anaesthetic and do a little stitching. It will hurt a trifle, but you will not mind that, eh?'

'No, doctor,' replied Troy, hoping it was true.

'If you do silly things like falling on to rocks then you expect to be hurt, eh?' The voice was gruff, but the eyes were kind.

'Yes, doctor,' concurred Troy obediently. She was beginning to like the little tubby doctor with his twinkling blue eyes and greying, tufty hair and moustache. 'I'm sorry to be such a nuisance to you,' she added, her voice a little wobbly.

The bushy brows twitched. 'Hm . . . it is what I am here for.' He bent over to give her the injection and her hand was taken suddenly in a firm grasp. She looked up, but Lucien was watching the doctor. After a moment her hand was released and she felt the absurd inclination to weep.

Dr Dubois set to work and during the next quarter of an hour chatted non-stop in French to Lucien. It was soothing to hear of Madame Tufre's twins and René Rousard's new wife, the state of the government and the proposed wealth tax, the lovely May weather and the growth of the vine and last, and most interesting of all, Lucien Charon's love life.

'How is it with the so beautiful Madeleine de Vesci, Lucien?'

'I went to Paris on business, Marcel.'

'But you allowed business to mix with pleasure, for a surety,' stated the doctor with a chuckle. Out of the corner of her eye Troy saw Lucien give her a brief look and his voice was amused as he gave a laconic: 'Naturally.'

'And when are you going to take Madame de Vesci to wife, Lucien? A lonely widow, sophisticated, intelligent, with a good dowry—what more do you want, man?'

'You're a meddling old fool, Marcel,' observed Lucien mildly.

'So you frequently tell me.' The doctor paused, frowned over his handiwork and then, face clearing, added: 'You are not the kind to live alone, Lucien.'

Lucien gave a derisive laugh. 'I hardly live alone, Marcel!'

'You should have a son,' the older man went on stubbornly.

'You are as bad as Grand'mère, and you both know that there is Philippe.'

'Accidents happen, as your father knew to his cost. Besides, every man wants a son.'

Lucien smiled, his face softening. 'You seem to have managed without one, Marcel.'

'Oh, I have been too busy . . . and you are all the son

I have ever wanted,' the doctor said gruffly. 'We speak only for your good, your grand'mère and I, boy. But you will go your own way, like your father before you. The bandage, please.' He looked across at Troy and said in English: 'We have nearly finished, young lady.' He hummed for a while, saying presently: 'You have been out shooting in the woods today, Lucien? Did you get anything?'

'Only the girl,' Lucien offered, and the doctor wheezed delightedly.

'She is a brave one. Where did this happen?' and he nodded to the wound he was now bandaging.

'She was paddling in the Sève, near the waterfall, and tumbled in. Hence our wet state.' Lucien looked at his watch.

'Patience, patience, we have nearly done. Surely you are not anxious to be rid of such a girl? Not like you, Lucien . . . consider that marvellous hair!'

'She's a termagant,' Lucien said calmly, and the doctor gave a bark of laughter.

'She has character as well as beauty, eh?'

Troy took a deep breath and turned her head, addressing the doctor politely in English. 'You have finished, Doctor?'

'Nearly, nearly . . . only the tetanus jab as a precaution.' He went about this in a businesslike manner, Troy hardly feeling a thing as he rubbed the skin on her upper arm briskly for a few seconds with a ball of cotton wool. No hand grip this time and Troy would have refused one. Termagant, indeed!

'There. All finished.' The doctor moved to the basin, shooing Lucien out of the way. With an air of almost boredom, Lucien crossed to the window.

Ignoring him, Troy half sat up, resting her weight on one elbow.

'Thank you, Dr Dubois. You must let me know your fee.' She saw Lucien make an impatient movement, saying curtly as he turned:

'I shall settle with Dr Dubois.'

'How kind of you to offer,' said Troy, wonderfully humble.

Lucien eyed her narrowly for a moment and said dismissively:

'I was just considering whether to advise you not to go wandering off on your own again. It is foolish, especially in a strange country, but I have decided against it. It is doubtful whether you would accept the advice.'

'You mean that ferocious dogs wander about loose all over France?' she asked innocently, enjoying the sudden tightening of his mouth, 'or perhaps I was trespassing? I saw no sign forbidding me entry . . .'

Dr Dubois was standing between them, drying his hands, looking from one to the other with obvious delight. Lucien broke in, with great control:

'There is no sign. The woods of Charon are free for any to walk.'

'I suppose I should be thankful that I didn't get shot at,' she observed, and received the suave reply:

'That would have been unlikely, Mademoiselle Maitland, unless you are capable of flying through the air.'

There was silence. Dr Dubois patted her shoulder. 'Do not let him put you down, young lady. Have you nothing further to say? He has always been used to his own way, that is the trouble.'

Lucien gave a bark of laughter. Troy said:

'If I antagonise Monsieur Charon too much, Doctor, I might find I have to walk back. I must be grateful that he hasn't accused me of being a witch on a broomstick,' and she swung her legs to the ground.

'No, no, we will keep off the leg, if you please, today,' scolded the doctor, pausing while writing instructions on a bottle of tablets. He handed it to her. 'Two tonight and then as necessary,' he told her, adding slyly: 'And now Lucien will carry you. He is a strong fellow and will enjoy the prospect.'

Lucien came forward. 'You must learn to ignore the good doctor's teasing, *mademoiselle*,' and lifting her once more into his arms he strode back along the passageway and out into the sunlight. 'I shall need to know where you are staying.'

Troy settled herself on the back seat. 'Yes, I'm sorry . . . I am with a Madame Marin at the farm just down the hill . . .'

'I know it.' Lucien stared at her oddly and then climbed into the driver's seat. He did not need to be directed to the Marin farm. The dog appeared again, barking furiously, until he saw who it was and then wagged his tail. César and Satan, extremely well-behaved, sat immobile in canine condescension. As Madame Marin came to the door, Troy said quickly:

'Will you ask Madame if she is still prepared to accept me as her guest now? I realise that for at least tomorrow I shall not be mobile and perhaps it will not be convenient. I don't wish to be a burden to her.'

'Modestine will be delighted to attend to you,' Lucien told her with annoying certainty and Troy replied with asperity:

'*I* don't know that, Monsieur Charon, and neither do *you*. Will you please be good enough to ask her?'

He swung himself down from the jeep and stood for a moment considering her, before saying soothingly:

'But naturally I shall ask her, if you wish it.' He

went to meet Madame Marin who, after an exchange of words, disappeared into the farmhouse. Lucien strode back, his eyes on Troy's enquiring face.

'As I supposed, Modestine is only too happy to be of help. You need not worry.' He smiled, a warm, generous smile, and his grey eyes were kindly. 'I can leave you with complete assurance. As a young boy I was always getting into scrapes with her son and know, to my good fortune, what an excellent nurse she makes.' His face changed to dismay as he saw Troy's brown eyes fill with sudden tears. '*Mon Dieu!* What have I said to upset you?' He leaned forward and gently smoothed away a tear that had spilled over and was trickling down her cheek. 'What a formidable opponent you are . . . and how underhand to use such a weapon.' He shook his head, a faint smile on his face. 'Tck, tck, what chance do you leave a poor fellow now?'

Troy gave a choking laugh and wiped her cheeks, childlike, with the sleeve of his sweater. She took a deep breath and said contritely:

'Monsieur Charon—I haven't behaved very well this afternoon, I'm sorry . . .'

The tips of his fingers touched her lips to stop the flow of words and he mocked gently:

'Come, come, Victoire . . . tears *and* an apology? You deal most unfairly!' He swung her down from the jeep. 'But I do not despair. It is only that now you are feeling a little fatigued after your ordeal with the Sève rocks. Tomorrow you will be happily crossing swords with me without compunction.' No more was said until he put her down on the pretty patchwork counterpane. Then Troy tentatively observed:

'Monsieur, don't you think that it's a coincidence, our meeting like this? I assure you that when we met in Paris I had no idea I should see you again.'

'Life is full of coincidences,' he agreed, looking down at her enigmatically. 'For me, however, it is not at all extraordinary. I live here.'

She stared at him, eyes widening in surprise. 'Here?' She gazed round uncertainly. 'In this farmhouse?'

He said impatiently: 'No, no . . . at Sève.' He paused. 'Whereas, you, on holiday, could have chosen anywhere to spend it, and yet you chose Sève.' It was casually said, but there was slight challenge in the grey eyes.

'Perhaps my choice of Sève was not so haphazard,' suggested Troy. She frowned, considering the situation. She had to ask someone about Bellevigne, why not Lucien Charon, who lived in the district? 'I'm not purely on holiday, Monsieur Charon. I'm looking for something, and perhaps you could help me find it.'

The sound of a motor was heard outside and Lucien turned his head and looked out of one of the windows, saying as he did:

'In what way can I be of assistance?'

'Could you help me to find a house called Bellevigne?' asked Troy hopefully, and a little shyly, and found that she was waiting almost apprehensively for his answer.

Lucien turned from the window. 'You say you are looking for a house?'

Troy nodded. 'Yes. I know nothing about it other than its name—Bellevigne, and that it's in or near Sève. Do you know it?'

He gazed at her thoughtfully. 'I can tell you about Bellevigne and take you there without difficulty. But may I ask the reason for your interest in the Château? There are much grander, larger châteaux of the Loire than Bellevigne. Why do we tempt you, Mademoiselle Maitland?'

Château? Troy wondered if she had heard him right. Footsteps could be heard clattering the stair and Madame Marin swept into the room, speaking in rapid French.

'Come, Monsieur le Comte, Mademoiselle should rest . . . here is some freshly made lemon tea for her to drink to soothe her. Also, Jean-Jacques has arrived and wishes to have a word with you.'

'Very well, Modestine, I shall leave the patient in your so capable hands. Dubois has prescribed some tablets . . . you will see that she takes them?'

'Assuredly, Monsieur le Comte.'

'Then I will go and see Jean-Jacques.' Lucien glanced at Troy who was staring blankly up at him, feeling as though she had received a body blow. He spoke in his excellent English: 'We shall talk of Bellevigne tomorrow when you will be feeling, hopefully, the benefit of a good night's rest. *À demain*, Mademoiselle Maitland.' He smiled and left the room. As soon as his footsteps faded, Troy asked urgently:

'Madame Marin . . . you . . . what did you call him?' She floundered and thrust fingers through her hair. 'I mean . . . I thought he said his name was Charon?'

Madame nodded. 'That is so. Charon is the family name.'

'But . . . you called him Monsieur le Comte!'

'That also is so. Lucien Valéry Charon, Comte de Sève,' acknowledged Madame Marin. She gestured to the window. 'Unfortunately you cannot see Bellevigne from here, the woods hide the Château. And now, would Mademoiselle allow me to find her night things? It would be preferable for you to take your evening meal in bed and perhaps you may manage a rest before then. It was an unfortunate accident to happen, but Dr Dubois is a good doctor.'

Troy hardly heard her. Comte de Sève! Château Bellevigne! No wonder all the villagers acknowledged him as they went through. No wonder he was walking the woods as though he owned them! Madame handed Troy her nightgown, saying:

'My husband runs the Home Farm for Monsieur le Comte, and my son, Jean-Jacques, is his right-hand man at the vineyards.'

'H—how interesting,' answered Troy feebly, thinking—vineyards! Charon wines!

'As far as the eye can see, and beyond, is de Sève property. Of course, the Château was only built on its present site during the eighteenth century.' Madame broke off as a call summoned her to the top of the stairs and on her return she said with satisfaction: 'Mademoiselle, you have no need to worry about your car. Jean-Jacques is going to fetch it for you. But first he must have the keys.'

'Yes, of course.' Troy opened her bag and found the keys. A small white card tucked into the side pocket triggered off a memory. She said slowly: 'I thought that Monsieur Charon was something to do with a banking house?'

Madame Marin nodded and replied with simple pride: 'Assuredly. There have been Charons connected with banking for five generations, *mademoiselle*, and the union of Descartes and Charon for three of them. Monsieur Lucien has studied and worked in the family bank—it is expected, you understand, and he is naturally a director. However, another branch of the family deals with the major running of the bank.'

'What a busy man he must be,' was all Troy could find to say, but it was enough. Madame replied with deep conviction:

'Monsieur Lucien is a good man, *mademoiselle*, and

a respected *patron.*' She took the offered keys. 'Do you need any assistance in preparing for bed, *mademoiselle*?'

Troy shook her head, smiling gratefully. 'No, thank you. I'm sure I can manage.'

'Very well, but if you need me you must call.' Madame eyed the bandaged leg critically, passing on to Troy's face. 'You are feeling the reaction to your little adventure. Rest now, and I will bring you a light meal later on.'

'You're very kind, *madame*, and I'm sorry your son has the trouble of fetching my car . . .'

'It is no trouble for Jean-Jacques, and Monsieur le Comte wishes it.' Madame gave the room one last swift appraisal and finding everything to her satisfaction, she hurried out.

Monsieur le Comte wishes it . . .

Troy lay back with a troubled laugh. It was all too confusing to make any sense. How on earth had her grandmother come to be mixed up with the de Sèves of Bellevigne? And what on earth was she to say to Lucien de Sève tomorrow? She pulled a face at the thought. Something like . . . I'm awfully sorry, Monsieur le Comte, but I came to Sève because I thought I'd inherited Bellevigne!

Very funny! However, pondering the mystery would not solve it and it was time she undressed and got into bed properly or else Madame would be up, scolding her . . . no doubt saying firmly that Monsieur le Comte wished it!

Troy sat rather wearily up and slowly peeled off the borrowed sweater. It was still warm from her body, and holding it pensively in her hands she found she liked the idea of wearing something of his, something that had touched his skin and still carried with it his unmistakable body smell. Liked the idea of mixing her own shape and smell with his.

She threw the sweater to the bottom of the bed, exasperation sweeping over her. She unzipped the jump-suit, and as she did so her cheeks grew warm as she remembered those grey eyes giving her the once-over, insultingly impersonal in their appraisal, and heard again the impatient 'Can you get that thing off?'

'I ought to have taken it off,' she muttered crossly, struggling out of it now with difficulty. 'That would have shown him!' and she paused in the fight, giving a strangled laugh, self-mockingly thinking that it would indeed! and rather more than propriety demanded! At last she was free of the jump-suit and with a new, critical awareness she studied herself in the angled mirror on the chest of drawers, seeing what Lucien de Sève would have seen . . . the tousled hair, a mass of rust waves and curls, the oval face, pale now with dark brown eyes predominant, the sloping shoulders, high firm breasts, flat stomach, curved hips and long legs.

With a grimace at her reflection Troy tossed the mutilated suit on to the floor. How silly to be mooning over what Lucien de Sève would have seen, or would have thought. She supposed, sarcastically, that he was familiar with the female shape and form and no doubt not starved of women's company.

By the time she had donned the nightgown and scrambled between the sheets she was glad to be in bed. Her body relaxed but her mind could not. She went over the events of the day, the encounter on the Descartes' balcony, her grandmother's involvement with Bellevigne, returning persistently to Lucien Valéry Charon, Comte de Sève.

His face seemed indelibly imprinted on the back of her lids. Annoyingly so. It was one thing to meet a man, briefly, at a party and be attracted, and quite another to come up against him in the cold, clear light of day. Especially in such a stupid manner, especially losing one's temper! Forget Lucien Charon and consider Lucien de Sève . . . quite another kettle of fish.

She stirred uneasily. Her breathing deepened and slowed. On the edge of sleep the thought drifted over her of what it would be like to be carried in his arms because he wanted her there and not out of a sense of duty . . .

CHAPTER THREE

'I HAVE come to take you to the Château, Mademoiselle Troy.'

It was after breakfast the following morning. The sun spilled in through the window of Madame Marin's 'best' room, and Troy was wondering what to do. Her thoughts had been struggling with what had happened the day before and by the time Jean-Jacques Marin arrived, she was all twisted up with the ironies of fate that had landed her in this odd and extremely embarrassing predicament.

Only one thing had she managed to salvage from her reflections—that it would be dangerous to become emotionally involved with Lucien de Sève, even in her thoughts. A quirk of chance had brought her back into his orbit. She would find out about her grandmother's connection with the de Sèves and then be on her way. She had work to do.

Jean-Jacques' arrival was a welcome respite from knowing what she should do and doing what she wanted to do.

He stood before her, an articulate, intelligent man in his late twenties, with a pleasant face. She had been expecting someone different from this immaculately dressed, composed man whose polite, rather formal manner reminded her that to be the estate manager of such a large and flourishing vineyard as the Charon Vineyard was a position that needed someone extremely competent.

He had obviously been given his orders this morning. Go and fetch Victoria Maitland and bring her to me. Just like that. Snap the fingers and come running.

A feeling of exasperated amusement swept over her. Since the Château was the very place she had travelled all this way to see, it would be ridiculous to refuse now, and shrugging aside the feeling that she was a puppet and Lucien master of the strings, she said innocently:

'I suppose it's a case of when Monsieur le Comte says "jump", we "jump"?' and wondered if the self-possessed, so earnest Jean-Jacques had a sense of humour.

'Monsieur Lucien is a busy man, *mademoiselle*. If you do not feel well enough this morning, I am sure he will understand.'

Not only had Jean-Jacques inherited his mother's hazel eyes, he had her reverence for Monsieur le Comte as well. It was what she would have expected of Lucien de Sève's 'right-hand man'. She said gravely:

'I'm sure I can manage . . . so long as I don't have to walk to the Château.'

Jean-Jacques looked relieved and horrified at the same time.

'I assure you there is no necessity to walk, *mademoiselle*! Everything is arranged for your comfort.' He smiled. 'Lucien considered the Beaufighter to be the most accommodating vehicle available, and as I do not often get the chance to drive it myself I am much obliged to you.'

'I'm glad you're pleased, but I haven't the remotest idea what a Beaufighter is,' Troy laughingly confessed.

'I shall show you.' He paused and asked diffidently: 'Will you allow me to carry you out?'

Troy eyed him with resignation. 'I walked down the

stairs this morning and I'm sure I can get to this Beaufighter, whatever it is, but I suppose Monsieur le Comte said I was not to walk?' She took pity on him and gave a cheerful sigh. 'Oh, very well. I should hate you to be shot for not obeying orders,' and her eyes danced with amusement.

Jean-Jacques did not seem as if he knew how to take her teasing. Perhaps Lucien de Sève was not allowed to be mocked? As he carried her through the farmhouse it was expected that Troy should recall someone else's arms, remember another occasion, and she said quickly:

'I understand from your mother that you live at the Château?'

'Yes. I have a set of rooms. It is more convenient for me to be on the spot,' acknowledged Jean-Jacques, and Troy added:

'You speak very good English.'

'Thank you. I have Lucien's father, Philippe de Sève, to thank for my education. Unfortunately, he was killed in a riding accident some ten years ago. It was a great shock to us all.'

'You have known Monsieur Lucien for a long time?'

'For all of my life, *mademoiselle*,' Jean-Jacques replied simply. He twisted sideways and negotiated the back door. 'There she is—the Bristol Beaufighter!' They crossed the yard and Troy looked with curiosity at the large, expensive-looking four-seater coupé parked beyond the gate. Incongruous against the farm setting, it stood, angular and distinctive, the cream bodywork and shining chrome sparkling in the sunshine. Difficult not to be impressed.

'It's a British car,' Jean-Jacques told her, setting her on her feet and opening the passenger door. 'It really is a splendid vehicle. Will you be comfortable in the front?'

Troy eyed a passenger seat that was as broad and as high as an armchair with enough leg room for a giant, and gave a laugh.

'I'm sure I shall be . . . we could hold a party in here.' While Jean-Jacques helped her in she glanced appreciatively round the walnut veneer and pale cream leather, and when he climbed in beside her, she went on: 'I bet she goes like the wind.'

He nodded. 'It is the power and speed that is useful. Lucien drives regularly to Paris and Bordeaux. Please connect the belt, Mademoiselle Troy. It is against the law in our country to drive without the seat-belt fastened.' He waited while this was done and then began to drive down the drive and out on to the road.

Troy could hardly hear the engine and they seemed to just glide along. She said:

'I can understand why you like to drive this, she goes like a dream.' Even while she spoke, she could tell that they were winding their way round the lower slopes of the Sève hill. 'Why is it called the Beaufighter?'

'The Bristol Aeroplane Company built a fighting machine called the Beaufighter in the last war and it has been named after that.' He threw her a quick grin, his face becoming, for an instant, boyish. 'I owe my place behind the wheel today to an important telephone call that Lucien was obliged to wait in for.' He nodded ahead. 'We're nearly there.'

Troy's eyes eagerly scanned their direction. Swinging through a walled boundary gateway, the tall iron gates open to accommodate them, the car left the rows of vines growing either side of the road. She caught sight of a pair of exotic stone beasts, wings outstretched, perched ominously on the gateposts as they passed, and then the drive curved and with increasing pulse rate she encountered her first view of the Château Bellevigne.

'Oh, it's beautiful!' She did not realise that she had spoken the words out loud until Jean-Jacques replied complacently:

'Yes, it is, isn't it?'

The Château was no Gothic or Baroque castle but rather a country mansion built on noble proportions. The sun was shining on the weathered stone, lighting it to good effect, and as they drove through the surrounding parkland and the Château drew nearer Troy could see that the architecture was of a style predominant in the eighteenth century, with Corinthian columns and traditional high roofs and slender chimneys. The forecourt, which fronted a flight of stone steps leading to the main entrance, was itself flanked by a curving stone balustrade, and centred by a fountain. The whole was backclothed by trees, and higher still, a sweep of vines, severely ridged, finally topped by Sève itself.

Troy was enchanted. Bellevigne was all, and more than, she could have wished for, and Lucien de Sève and his way of life more unapproachable. It was almost a relief.

Jean-Jacques negotiated the gentle curve of the drive round the fountain, and ignoring the main entrance, turned the corner to pull slowly to a halt at a side door.

'This is the office wing, my rooms are above.' he explained as he helped her out. He carried her into the Château, halting at a beautifully carved door, slightly ajar. Shouldering it open, he went into the room beyond.

Bookshelves, pictures, polished wood, crystal decanters and glasses on silver trays met Troy's swivelling gaze. Dominating the room was a desk, the surface neatly organised but dominated by three telephones. Lucien de Sève came round the desk to meet them. He was dressed in a dark suit and looked every inch a Count. A ripple of unease gripped Troy. Each time she met him he seemed a different person. To date this man was the most formidable.

His voice was polite, his expression enigmatic. '*Bonjour*, Mademoiselle Maitland. I hope Jean-Jacques has looked after you well?' He took her hand in a firm greeting. His touch showed that nothing was changed. The unease deepened into panic.

'He has been splendid,' replied Troy, her enthusiasm surprising even herself, but it sprang from an instinctive desire to cover up. She turned her head to smile, hoping her eyes did not mirror her panic, and added directly to Jean-Jacques: 'And most kind.' Now there were two enigmatic faces. Poor Jean-Jacques!

Lucien said smoothly: 'Good. I can always rely upon Jean-Jacques to be a most accomplished emissary. Now, where shall we put you? The wing-chair, I think, Jean-Jacques, with the footstool.' He waited while she was made comfortable. 'That's all for the moment, Jean-Jacques. I'll ring if I want you.'

Jean-Jacques gave Troy a polite: '*À bientôt*, Mademoiselle Troy,' and left the room, closing the door softly behind him. Before either of them could speak, the telephone rang and while Lucien answered it Troy sat quietly, absorbing the atmosphere. She guessed there was nothing false about this room. It was totally in character with this Lucien de Sève, just as the world-weary cynic of the Descartes' party and the countryman of yesterday were real. She heard him say a crisp: 'Send him along when he's ready,' and then he was crossing the beautiful Aubusson carpet and leaning against the front of the desk, arms straight, hands gripping the edge. His hands had been almost the first thing she had noticed about him—strong and lean with neat, rounded nails and no rings.

'You had an easy night, I trust?' he asked.

Troy lifted her eyes from his hands to his face. 'Yes, thank you.'

'Good. You took the painkillers that Marcel Dubois prescribed?'

A sense of humour came to one's aid in the most unlikely situations. Troy's eyebrows rose a fraction.

'But of course. Madame Marin would have felt that she had failed in her duty if I had not. She stood over me while I swallowed them down and when the deed was done she could then relax. Monsieur le Comte's orders had been obeyed.'

His lips twitched slightly as he contemplated her innocent face.

'Hm ... And you are comfortable at the Home Farm?'

She was able to answer truthfully and enthusiastically. 'Very. The Marins are most kind, and the food is excellent.'

Lucien nodded, his face softening. 'I'm glad, but not surprised. Modestine has filled many a lonely boy's stomach with her delicious yeast buns and newly baked bread in her day.'

Troy had the fleeting image of a dark-haired little boy, living in the large Château, going over to the Home Farm for some motherly love and comfort. She squashed the picture as quickly as it came. He need not have been speaking of himself, and it would not do to confuse the vulnerable little boy with this self-assured adult.

'Monsieur le Comte . . .' Troy began, when he interrupted her.

'What is all this Monsieur le Comte business? Yesterday you were quite happy with Monsieur Charon, and I believe you did not find Lucien difficult on the Descartes' balcony.'

Troy felt her cheeks grow warm. 'What happened there was not usual. If you remember, it was your birthday, and I was feeling . . .' she struggled for a word, '. . . charitable.' It was the best she could do on the spur of the moment.

Again, his lips twitched. 'Ah, charitable!' He gave a shrug. 'But even so, as I have rescued you from two unfortunate incidents, I consider we have a bond which precludes formality.'

Oh, you do, do you? thought Troy grimly. Well, that bond is too dangerous, Monsieur le Comte, and your title makes a good barrier! She replied equably:

'I have to thank you for sending your magnificent Beaufighter to bring me here. It is most impressive.'

A flicker of annoyance passed over his face. 'My dear girl, I did not intend it to impress you. It was the most comfortable . . .' A knock sounded on the door and he called: 'Come in. Ah, Marcel, *bonjour* . . .'

Doctor Dubois exchanged a greeting and then looked critically at Troy.

'Good morning, *mademoiselle*, and how are you feeling today?' The bushy brows met and giving her no time to answer, he went on briskly: 'I shall be obliged if you would send for Zenobie, Lucien. She is aware I shall need her and should be close by.' He began to unwind the bandage and as the wound was revealed gave a grunt of satisfaction. 'Good, good . . . coming along nicely. Ah, Zenobie, you have my bag, thank you.'

Troy looked up to find an elderly woman standing beside him. Grey hair was caught back into a bun; thin and straight-backed, she could have been any age over sixty. Troy smiled at her tentatively and received a quiet: '*Bonjour, mademoiselle*,' in return.

Lucien had cut himself off from the trio, his back towards them as he answered the telephone. For this, Troy was grateful. She had chosen to wear a simple, sleeveless blouse and a floral full skirt, the soft material of the skirt being the most comfortable for her injured leg. For the doctor to redress the wound it was necessary to show a large expanse of bare leg, and here, in this businesslike atmosphere, she was gripped with a ridiculous sense of embarrassment. She wanted to clear up something else that gave her misgivings and asked persuasively:

'I do hope you're going to allow me to walk on this leg of mine, Doctor?'

He worked in silence for a moment, Zenobie passing him his requirements, and replied bluntly:

'So long as you use the sense the good Lord gave you. Not too much today, and then resting when necessary. Thank you, Zenobie, that will be all. Tell Madame la Comtesse I shall be with her in a few minutes.' Zenobie silently left the room. The doctor continued to re-bandage his patient's leg and while doing so lapsed into his own language, saying:

'I saw Philippe briefly as I came in. How is he?'

Lucien shrugged. 'Bored. Looking for trouble.'

'His mother suffocates the lad. He should be at school. I tell her that his delicate days are over and that he needs the company of other boys his age, but my advice goes for nought.'

'It is difficult,' stated Lucien, frowning. 'Grand'-

mère sits in isolation in her rooms, pretending to know and see nothing, but knows and sees everything, Zenobie being her ears and eyes. You realise, Marcel, that my hands are virtually tied.' He gave an exasperated sigh and swung round, abandoning that line of conversation. 'You will be taking sherry with Grand'mère before you go?'

Doctor Dubois straightened, his task finished. 'It will be my pleasure.'

It was Troy who was now gazing out of the window, trying to dissociate herself with the talk going on around her. She was growing decidedly uneasy about her deception and decided to confess she could understand French at the first favourable opportunity. She would look a fool, but that seemed to be the role she was destined to play for Lucien de Sève.

'I shall tell your grandmother,' the doctor was saying as he crossed the room and entered another, the sound of running water accompanying his words, 'that the girl's injury is promising to heal nicely and that you will soon be absolved of all responsibility. I think Madame fears our visiting beauty has captivated your eye! You know her love of the English and what her thoughts on that would be!'

Out of the corner of her eye Troy could see him standing in the doorway, drying his hands. She also sensed that Lucien de Sève was watching her. The doctor chuckled, disappearing again, his voice wafting through teasingly:

'You have reassured her, I hope, Lucien, and told her you consider the girl to be a termagant?'

Troy consigned the drunken Georges to the devil and wished she had never begun this stupid charade. A casual glance told her that the pair of grey eyes were still resting upon her with steady appraisal and it was necessary to find great interest in a picture on the wall.

'You may tell Grand'mère that she need not worry,' Lucien drawled. 'Would you say, Marcel, that our termagant is a virgin?'

'Never can tell these days, Lucien,' replied the doctor with gruff humour. He appeared once more and made for his medical case. 'Shouldn't think so. Too pretty. Are you looking for a virgin, my boy? Going to be difficult, eh? You'll have to seek a young, untamed filly.' He eyed the young man slyly. 'There's one I can think of—your grandmother approves of her, as you well know.' He slapped his hat briskly against his leg. 'I'm going. Take care, Lucien.' He turned to Troy, saying in English: 'Goodbye, young lady. I'll see you in ten days to take out the stitches, if you're still around. If you intend to leave I'll give you a letter for your own doctor,' and giving her a quick handshake he bustled out of the room.

Lucien waited until the door closed and speaking in his own language he said conversationally:

'You'll still be around, Mademoiselle Maitland, I'm quite sure. What do you think?'

Her voice choked with indignant anger, Troy replied in her excellent French:

'Good manners prevent me from telling you!'

'You surprise me. I did not realise it was good manners to listen in on conversations on the pretence of non-comprehension.'

'That wasn't my fault,' flared Troy, incensed at the injustice of his rebuke. She began to struggle up from the chair.

'Sit down. I have no intention of allowing you to go yet.' The grey eyes were cold, the face a blank mask.

Troy's lip curled. 'Bully, as well as . . .' she searched frantically for a suitable French word and spat it out,

'... slimy reptile!' She sank back and glared accusingly. 'You baited me on purpose! You were perfectly outrageous just to see if I would react!'

'And I succeeded, didn't I? I merely wished to test my suspicions, and it was fairly obvious that you could understand what I was saying. You jumped a mile and that maidenly blush was quite something . . . I thought them to be out of date.' His eyes narrowed. 'I can understand why termagant might cause the bristles to rise, but virgin?' He quirked a brow, his voice cool. 'In this day and age?'

'It's not what you said,' retorted Troy, stung, 'but the cat-and-mouse way you went about it.'

'I only had suspicions ... and no insult was intended. I could, I assure you, have embarrassed you even more, had I chosen.'

'I'm sure you could have, *monsieur*. Your imagination and expertise must be vast!' retaliated Troy scathingly. 'I had no intention of pretending I couldn't understand, and it was all Georges's fault ...' She stopped short and bit her lip, vexed. 'I was going to tell you, anyway,' she added impatiently.

'I'm very glad to hear it.' He paused and went on thoughtfully: 'Georges's fault . . . ah, yes, now it comes back to me. Something to do with a man being happy in your arms, was it not? And the delightful assertion that my bed would not be cold with you in it.'

'Heaven forbid! I'd sooner sleep in the fields,' Troy observed icily.

Lucien smiled sardonically, his look shrewd and ironic. 'You misjudge Bellevigne and myself, Mademoiselle Maitland.'

With face aflame, Troy demanded impetuously: 'Have you finished? May I now go, Monsieur le Comte?' His title was voiced with exaggerated politeness.

'By no means. We have only touched the tip of the iceberg . . .' Lucien looked up with a frown as the door burst open and a boy flung himself into the room. He was in a white-hot rage and could hardly get his words out.

'Lucien! Patrice says you've given orders that I'm not to ride Sable!'

'Good morning, Philippe. Do I have to remind you yet again that it is the custom to knock on this door before entering?'

'But Sable, Lucien! You know I can manage him!' Philippe declared passionately.

'You are over-optimistic, Philippe. When you have closed the door, perhaps you will say good morning to Mademoiselle Maitland?' There was an edge of steel in Lucien's voice and eye which finally got through. Philippe turned abruptly and closed the door and then looked sullenly over to where Troy was sitting. Lucien said: 'Mademoiselle Maitland, my half-brother, Philippe. Philippe, Mademoiselle Maitland is from England, but she speaks excellent French, so you will not have to practise your English on us at the moment.'

Troy felt a stab of pity for the boy, although she knew he probably deserved his brother's recrimination. He was a good-looking youth, or would have been had his expression been sunnier. He was as fair as Lucien was dark but had his build and what she was to come to recognise as the de Sève nose.

'Good morning, Philippe,' Troy said kindly, giving him a smile. He was not to be mollified nor side-tracked.

'Good morning.' He allowed her a sweeping glance and turned back to his brother. 'Patrice says I mayn't ride in the mornings. Lucien! Do you hear?'

'I hear, and imagine Grand'mère can also. Please control yourself, Philippe. Either say your piece in a reasonable manner or leave.'

Philippe flushed but stood his ground. 'Did you give those orders?'

Lucien eyed him fully for some seconds, saying at last: 'Yes.'

'Lucien, how could you?' burst out Philippe. 'You've allowed Maman to persuade you . . .'

'Your mother is naturally concerned over Sable. The rest is my doing. Until you show some improvement in your studies, Philippe, you will not ride in the mornings. You've abused your privileges and cannot be trusted any more.' Lucien paused and said more kindly: 'Come, Philippe, admit that you have been neglecting your books. Is that fair to your tutor? A man whose living depends upon you? You take your examinations next year. What sort of chance will you have if you do not work? No decisions will be made about your future until your formal education is over. Do you hear me, Philippe?'

'Yes! I hear you!' The words were venomously spoken, and swinging violently on his heel, Philippe stormed out of the room, banging the door behind him.

The silence left behind seemed weighted with words. Lucien stared hard at the door for some seconds before turning to frown out of the window, hands in pockets, shoulders slightly hunched.

Troy sat waiting. At last he turned, saying abruptly: 'I'm sorry you were subjected to that.'

She said quietly: 'I'm sorry too . . . you would have preferred being alone.'

He gave a brusque laugh. 'You will learn, *mademoiselle*, that Philippe cares nothing for keeping his grievances to himself. That outburst was a minor one, believe me.' He walked back to the desk and hitched himself on the corner, looking down at her. 'Now, where were we? Ah, yes, I remember . . . any advance on slimy reptile? I must congratulate you on your accent, it is excellent.'

Grey eyes held brown for a long moment.

Troy looked down at her hands in her lap. 'I'm afraid you bring out the worst in me.'

'I do seem to have the unlucky knack, do I not?'

Was there a hint of amusement in his voice? Her lashes flew up.

'I should have told you—you're quite right. But once you'd assumed, it was difficult. I can only repeat that a confession was trembling on my lips and would have been made today,' and this last was said with a slight uplift of the chin.

Lucien folded his arms across his chest. Troy could see a handsome gold wristwatch and the glint of gold cuff links. There was a tiny white scar across the knuckles of his left hand.

'And have you any other confessions trembling on those lips of yours?'

Troy's eyes widened as they searched his face.

'For instance, why you were looking for Bellevigne?' His tone was almost offhand.

She stared in consternation. Incredible though it seemed, she had been so busy reacting to the man she had forgotten the real purpose of her visit. Her lips parted and closed. Where on earth to start?

'Is it so difficult?' he asked mildly.

Troy brushed her lips with the tip of her tongue and gave a half laugh. 'Yes, it is.'

He leaned forward, encouragingly. 'Try me,' he urged.

She shrugged. 'It sounds preposterous, and I know so little about . . .' She broke off. She remembered the slight emphasis on the word 'confessions' and said slowly: 'You know exactly why I'm here, don't you? You know who I am and . . .' She stopped and drew a deep breath. 'You really are the most aggravating man! How long have you known?'

Lucien pursed his lips, replying calmly: 'About you, personally? A few moments ago. About your grandmother—we were informed of her death some days back. However, we were under the impression that your mother was still alive.'

'Both my parents were killed in a train derailment when I was eleven and my grandmother, then a widow, brought me up. You say, a few moments ago . . .?'

'After your illuminating question yesterday as to the whereabouts of a house called Bellevigne I realised you were probably related to Victoria Courtney. Early this morning I rang through to my lawyers who, in turn, got in touch with London. My lawyers rang me back a few moments ago while Marcel was attending you, and they confirmed my suspicions.'

Troy grimaced in dismay at the word 'suspicions'. 'Look, I'm completely in the dark about all this. I didn't even know that Bellevigne existed until after Grandmother's death. I don't know why she's connected with the Château, or why money has been coming from France all these years. Please believe me . . .'

'I do,' he replied mildly.

She was amazed and showed it. 'You do?'

'No other member of my family is aware of your grandmother's existence, or your own. I, as eldest son, inherited the knowledge from my father, who, in his turn, was told by his father.'

'I see,' said Troy, not seeing at all.

'And being a curious young lady you decided to find out for yourself instead of waiting for your lawyers to unravel the thread.'

She nodded. 'I had a holiday due and had to come to Paris . . .'

'. . . for a photographic session,' broke in Lucien. 'You seem surprised. It is quite simple. I asked Armand Descartes who you were.'

There was a pause and then the implication of his words swept over her and the blood rushed to her cheeks. She said a feeble:

'Oh, did you?'

His eyes gleamed. 'I dislike receiving "charitable" birthday gifts only knowing the donor name.' He looked at his watch and stood up. 'I see it's very close to lunch. I hope I can persuade you to stay and eat with us. I promise to tell you all I know about your grandmother afterwards. Can you wait that long?'

'I've remained in ignorance for so long, a little longer isn't going to make much difference,' observed Troy with a grin, and his brows quirked.

'Remarkable patience and almost unknown in a woman.'

She gave him a very level look. 'Spoken like the true cynic!' She allowed him to help her up. 'I shall walk—Doctor Dubois said I may.' She eyed him defiantly. 'Either I walk on my own two feet or I go hungry.'

'Feet it shall be,' he returned smoothly, and gestured to the door that the doctor had used. 'There are a few letters I must sign. Perhaps you would like to freshen up while I do them?'

Troy found herself in a shower-cloakroom and was grateful for his thoughtfulness. Washing her hands, she lifted her eyes to the mirror and saw bright red cheeks and sparkling eyes. She splashed water on her face to try and cool it, but the warmth came from within. In Lucien de Sève's presence she seemed charged with an inner energy, and while this excited her, stimulated her, it also gave rise to an underlying uneasiness. She dragged the comb through her hair, trying to tame it into some semblance of neatness, but it bristled with electricity. Like me, she thought ruefully, quickly applying cologne to her wrists. I either bristle with antagonism or collapse into a shambles of apologies. She took a deep breath and rejoined him. He was sitting, writing, at the desk, but stood and came round to meet her.

'Ready?' he asked. 'Then we'll go in search of lunch. Are you going to accept the help of my arm, or does your independence balk at even that?' The grey eyes quizzed her.

Troy's lips curved. 'Not at all, Monsieur le Comte,' and she slipped her hand through the offered arm, grateful for his help. They walked slowly in deference to her limp, leaving the office and turning deeper into the Château. Lucien observed whimsically:

'You say Monsieur le Comte delightfully, but do you know, I think I prefer to hear Lucien on your lips?'

Troy's eyes danced. 'Oh, I can manage Lucien, if you insist, but Monsieur le Comte appeals to me so much more.'

An amused wariness crept into his voice. 'Dare I ask why?'

'I've never met a real live Count before. It does my ego good.'

He threw back his head and laughed. 'What a set-down!' he mourned, and then the amusement was replaced by one of politeness as he went on: 'Ah, here is Isabeau.'

Troy looked up to see the woman who had interrupted them on the Descartes' balcony coming towards them. She made to withdraw her arm, but Lucien, sensing her intention, tightened his grip slightly and she was forced to remain as she was. That brief glimpse of Isabeau was now confirmed. She was attractive and impeccably groomed, slim and petite, with thick blonde hair coiled in a knot, and the well-cut linen suit she was wearing was Paris-bought. As they drew nearer their steps halted.

Lucien said: 'Isabeau, this is Victoria Maitland, on holiday from England. You remember I spoke of her unfortunate accident yesterday? I considered the least we could do would be to ask her to lunch, and we are on our way there now. Victoire, I would like you to meet Isabeau de Sève, my stepmother.'

Troy hoped that her start of surprise at this astonishing news did not show. Lucien's stepmother? But Isabeau only looked a handful of years older, if that! Hardly old enough to be Philippe's mother, although she undoubtedly was—the likeness was apparent.

As Troy held out her hand she could see that Isabeau recognised her. The polite smile on Isabeau's lips did not quite reach her eyes, although her voice was friendly enough as she murmured a greeting.

Lucien offered Isabeau his other arm, saying: 'If you're in to lunch today, Isabeau, will you join us?' and they all three began to walk again, passing through a series of corridors and ante-rooms, all beautifully in period, with picture-lined walls and windows giving an occasional view of an inner courtyard or sweeping expanse of green parkland.

The conversation turned to Philippe and Isabeau said:

'Lucien, thank you for banning Sable. Philippe can be quite impossible at times, as we both know, and that horse petrifies me. I'm so terribly afraid that Philippe will have an accident like his father.'

'You'll not be able to keep Philippe away from horses entirely, Isabeau,' pointed out Lucien reasonably, 'but we'll do our best to keep him off Sable.'

'Do you ride, Mademoiselle Maitland?' Isabeau asked, and Troy replied enthusiastically:

'Yes, I do, whenever I can.'

'What a pity your injury will prevent you taking advantage of the excellent de Sève stables,' sympathised Isabeau, and Lucien observed:

'We must try and persuade her to stay long enough to do so.'

Troy shot him a startled look and there was an odd pause which she finished by saying quickly:

'What a beautiful home you have. You must be very proud of it.'

At this, Lucien glanced her way, a faint smile on his lips. 'I'm glad it pleases you. It has been in the family for a few centuries and with good luck will continue for a few more.' He stood aside, and Troy followed Isabeau through a door and gave an exclamation of appreciation at the room they had now entered. Lucien held a chair for Isabeau to be seated, while Jean-Jacques, who had risen at their entrance and smiled and murmured a greeting, did the same for Troy. Lucien caught her eye over the table.

'You like the Salle Ovale?' He gave a swift look round the room and went on with wry amusement: 'I have always felt grateful that Boffrand could only find the time to turn his talents to this one room. To have the whole of Bellevigne Rococo would strain my appreciation to the full.'

Troy laughed at his comical grimace. The Salle Ovale was the most ornate interior she had seen so far and was, as Lucien stated, decorated in the Rococo style. Flowers, nymphs, delicate leafwork were evident in the panels and ceiling as well as on the furniture, and a magnificent chandelier hung from the centre of the domed ceiling. Gilt and pastel colours made the room light, helped by the arched windows emphasing its oval shape.

Troy asked curiously: 'You prefer Classical architecture?'

Lucien nodded. 'I have to admit that I do. Baroque and Rococo are too fussy for my taste.' He stopped speaking to watch Philippe come in, mutter an almost inaudible apology for being late, and seat himself at the far end of the oval table. Lucien turned his eye from his brother and observed generally: 'Mademoiselle Maitland has an art degree tucked under her belt, so we have a guest who can really appreciate the finer points.'

Isabeau lifted her brows, spoon poised above the delicious onion soup which a young maid had just served.

'Really?' There was the slightest note of incredulity in the word. Jean-Jacques' expression was of friendly interest, Philippe showed none, friendly or otherwise. Isabeau went on, puzzled:

'Forgive me, but I thought Lucien mentioned that you were a photographer's model?'

The question was delicately put. Troy would have been amused had she been giving Isabeau her full attention, but she was too busy trying to remember if she had told Lucien about her art degree. Isabeau now gave an embarrassed smile, murmuring:

'I must have been mistaken.'

'Not at all, Isabeau,' assured Lucien, 'but Mademoiselle Maitland has now given up that job and is going to concentrate on what she has been trained for. She is one of England's up-and-coming names—a sculptress, a most talented young lady.'

A meat and salad platter was being transferred from a side table to the dining table. The disturbance broke the conversation for a moment and helped to conceal Troy's astonishment at this amazing statement.

She stared across the table at her host to meet his cool, enigmatic gaze, her thoughts in a whirl. How on earth had he learned that? And the praise! That was even more embarrassing. She looked down at her plate, confused. Could nothing be hidden from this man? At the lift of the telephone, could he find out anything he wanted to know? Such power was frightening.

She was aware that he had risen, was moving round the table, now filling the glasses. His murmured 'Charon, of course,' brought a quick, nervous answering smile to her lips, and the flickering of her eyes round the table. Almost of their own volition they lifted, were caught and held by Lucien's grey ones, in thoughtful regard upon her.

A nerve fluttered in her throat and when Jean-Jacques spoke Troy thankfully turned to him, still very conscious of the disconcerting man opposite.

CHAPTER FOUR

'I'VE asked for coffee to be served in here,' said Lucien, opening another beautifully carved door and gesturing for Troy to go in. 'We shall, I hope, be undisturbed long enough to unravel our mystery.'

The room was principally a library and had a masculine air of comfort about it. Troy looked round and, turning, found him watching her. 'Your room,' she stated, and he gave a slight smile.

'I wonder why you say that? Quite true, in fact.' He waited while she seated herself and drew forward a long tapestried footstool, easing it beneath her leg. He then began to competently pour the coffee, already set on a nearby low table.

Troy answered: 'It's essentially a man's room . . . wood panelling, books, few ornaments . . . and I spy a stereo unit tucked away in the corner. Altogether a snug retreat.' She smiled her thanks as he passed her the coffee and went on rather shyly: 'You have a beautiful home, Lucien.'

'But not everyone's ideal place to live. It has its drawbacks. We don't officially open up to the public, but if anyone is interested enough to seek us out we always show them round the main block.' He gave a wry smile. 'Thank the Lord the style for specialised rooms had come along by the time Bellevigne was built. Most are a reasonable size and make modern living in them a viable proposition. The main part of the Château is kept in period, but the rooms we use daily we've compromised . . . there's nothing particularly comfortable about eighteenth-century chairs . . . or beds.'

It was an obvious afterthought and said casually, but Troy was vividly reminded of their clash earlier and his taunt that she should not underestimate either the beds of Bellevigne or himself. The chance to test the beds was remote, but the more she was in his company, the more she realised that Lucien de Sève was most definitely not to be underestimated. She asked quickly:

'Who was the architect?'

'Jacques-Ange Gabriel—you've heard of him?—although some of the interiors were commissioned to other designers. It's been renovated several times, we're finding it a continuing process, luckily escaping the cannons, bombs and shells of a few wars. Its simple classical style has weathered the years, I think.'

'Indeed it has,' agreed Troy.

The grey eyes rested on her pensively. 'You really do like the place, don't you? As I say, not everyone's idea of home, but when you've been born to it you accept all the disadvantages. Now, suppose you tell me about your grandmother.' He took a stance near the fireplace.

Troy thought for a moment and began matter-of-factly: 'I'm named after her, as you know. When you're a child you take so much for granted. Bringing up a child of eleven in her early seventies couldn't have been easy, but she never made me aware of the fact. She was extremely intelligent and a firm believer in independence. I suppose I've always been a little in awe of her, for she was rather old-fashioned in her ways and outlook, and strict too. Yet she didn't ever try and influence me in any decisions . . . merely gave me her support. She was eighty-five when she died and it was only towards the end, when she was suddenly very ill, that she spoke of Bellevigne . . . in her ramblings, you understand. I had the feeling she was trying to tell me something that was important to her. Unfortunately, she left it too late.' Her throat closed up in an emotional lump and she had to stop. Lucien remained silent, looking down at her, an elbow resting against the mantle. After a moment Troy was able to go on, giving a tremulous smile. 'Strange how the realisation that you won't see someone again hits you at odd times. I thought I'd come to terms with it. She had had a long, full life, and was, I think, happy. Anyway . . . her solicitor told me that part of her income came from France, from a house called Bellevigne. You know the rest.' She had been staring at the coffee in her cup and now lifted her eyes to his, an odd, worried look on her face. 'Why did the money come from Bellevigne, Lucien, and why is my grandmother connected with your family?'

'I'll tell you all I know, but don't get uptight about it, will you? It happened a long time ago.' Lucien put down his cup and walked to a group of photographs, taking down one particular one and bringing it back to her, saying: 'My grandparents, Valéry and Claudine. Claudine is still alive, living in the south wing, and coming up for her eightieth birthday.' He moved away, leaving Troy still holding the sepia photograph containing double oval mounts. 'Valéry was twenty-three at the outbreak of the first world war. He joined the army, became an officer, and met your grandmother some time, I believe, in 1916 when she was over here nursing. Part of the Château was turned into a military hospital, and on brief spells of leave over the next two years Valéry became committed to the pretty English nurse.' He stopped. 'She was pretty, wasn't she? I'm only guessing. There's no photograph of her.' He was smiling slightly.

Troy nodded. 'Yes, she was pretty.'

The smile deepened. 'Yes, I thought she must have been. It was inevitable, don't you think, that they fell in love? Your Victoria Courtney and my Valéry de Sève? They were young, she was pretty, he was handsome, and both were vulnerable. Certainly during those terrible months when men were dying all around him Valéry must have clung to this girl's love with the tenacity of a lifeline. In August 1918 Valéry de Sève was reported missing, presumed dead, and two months later Victoria Courtney was sent back to England. She would have stayed, had Valéry been alive, and married him. You can imagine the loss and desolation she must have felt at the death of her lover.'

Troy had been engrossed in the story and while listening, was studying the photograph of Valéry. She saw a grave-faced man with Lucien's eyes and mouth and could understand her grandmother falling for the sensitive, almost poetic quality that was predominant in his features. Not readily a fighting man, she had been thinking, when Lucien's words penetrated. She looked up, startled.

'Lover?' She looked at him uncertainly and Lucien said gently:

'Oh, yes, I think so. It would not have happened under normal circumstances, but during wartime happiness is snatched with greedy hands. I doubt my grandfather would have felt so committed afterwards unless they had been lovers.' His eyes twinkled. 'Does that shock you?'

'No, of course not,' protested Troy. 'It takes a bit of getting used to, that's all. If you'd known my grandmother you would understand.' Her eyes shot to his, startled again. 'Afterwards? Do you mean . . .?'

'Life's not fair, is it? My grandfather had not died. He'd been wounded badly and, at first, not expected to live. After several weeks he returned to Bellevigne, still a sick man, to find that everyone thought him to be dead, including Victoria, who was no longer there. He instigated a search for her, and reports came back from England that she was married.'

'To my grandfather,' broke in Troy, 'but what could he expect? She could hardly mourn him for ever, could she? I can't remember my grandfather, he died when I was five, but from what I know of my mother's childhood, I think they were happy together. He was a lot older than Grandmother and a long-standing family friend. She probably drifted into it.' She handed over the photograph and reflected softly: 'Valéry must have been a kind man, to want to look after her the way he did. He must have loved her very much.'

Lucien replaced the photograph. 'This part of de Sève history, as I told you earlier, is not known among the family. I've often wondered if Grand'mère knows, but she's never said anything. Valéry waited three years before marrying her. He was thirty, she eighteen. He needed an heir.'

Troy found herself saying: 'But you don't intend to emulate him.'

Lucien shrugged and returned to sit down in the chair opposite her. 'Every man, if he's honest, likes to feel that something of himself lives on after him, but I think I'm too old to change my ways and I've never found anyone to make me want to. The situation here isn't a bed of roses and neither would being married to me be, either. The de Sève line is not broken. There is Philippe. He is still my father's son.' He gave a twisted smile. 'Every now and again Grand'mère renews her attempts to find me a wife. Invitations have gone out for her birthday celebration, we're opening up the *salle de banquet* and giving a ball, and no doubt I shall find included several eligible females whom Grand'mère will push forward hopefully.'

And the young girl, the one Doctor Dubois had spoken of, would she be there too? wondered Troy. She *would* be, of course! ... especially as Madame Claudine approved.

'Do these eligible females have any say in the matter?' she asked lightly, and his tone was ironic.

'I'm supposed to be a good catch.' He reached for a cigar box. 'Do you mind if I smoke? Let me refill your cup—the coffee is good, is it not?' He continued talking while performing this task, still in a mocking manner. 'The silly creatures are dazzled by the Château and the title and do not realise that independence sits a lot more comfortably than unhappy bondage. There are more arranged marriages in our country even today than you probably think.'

'Do you preclude the word love in all this?'

'Oh, love! If you believe in love then anything is possible,' he said dryly. 'And you, Victoire, is there someone waiting for you, back in England? This Hal Lindsey, for instance?'

'There are other things for women besides marriage,' Troy replied a trifle curtly.

'Of course there are,' he agreed mildly, 'and you have your work, we must talk about that some other time. There is still the question of how you prefer the payments to continue. For example, a quarterly ...'

'Surely the payments cease on my grandmother's death?'

Lucien raised his brows at her surprise. 'Why do

you suppose that? For legal reasons the money credited to your grandmother over the years has derived from a strip of Estate land on the south side, a slice of vineyard, a patch of woodland and some rather poor pasture. There's a cottage which used to belong to one of the gamekeepers but is now . . .'

'A cottage!' breathed Troy, her hands clasped in excitement. 'How marvellous!' She broke off as he shook his head, raising a hand to stem the flow.

'Please, I beg of you, Victoire, not to get excited. Only the shell of this cottage remains. I'm sorry if you suddenly envisaged yourself a property owner.'

'What a pity!' Troy gave a soft laugh and shrugged. 'For two minutes I thought I had a house of my very own over here.'

'That would please you?' questioned Lucien, gazing at her narrow-eyed through cigar smoke.

Troy deliberated. 'Yes, it would. I must have inherited my grandmother's love of France more deeply than I first realised.'

'Tell me how you come to have such a good knowledge of our language.'

She inclined her head at the compliment. 'I had a flair for languages in general, but it was Grandmother who insisted I keep the French going. Almost as if she knew I'd be needing it.'

'Which she did,' observed Lucien. He hesitated momentarily and proceeded with his customary air of cool detachment: 'I think it would be a good idea if you became aware of some of our more recent family history.' He crossed an immaculately trousered leg over the other and went on: 'You are too polite to touch upon the youthfulness of my stepmother.' He waved a hand to a pair of portraits either side of the mantle. 'My father, Philippe, and my mother . . . I never knew her, she died in childbirth.'

Troy studied the portraits in silence. Philippe de Sève was dressed in the uniform of a French army officer in the second world war. He had a stronger, more virile face than his father, Valéry, although there was, again, a keen likeness around the eyes . . . those clear, cool grey eyes. There was an energy and zest for life that the formal pose could not subdue, which he had passed on to both his sons, reflected Troy. Her eyes moved over to Lucien's mother. There was a frailty about her that was beautiful in its own way. On the calm, serene face there was the beginnings of a smile. There was more than a hint of Lucien in that smile. She looked gentle and very feminine.

Troy removed her gaze and said at last: 'I can see that you are their son.'

He moved position and reached for an ashtray. 'Shall I go on? I'm not boring you?' He accepted her 'Please do, I'm interested,' and leaned back, eyes almost closed, voice ruminative. 'Nothing of outstanding importance occurred until I was sixteen. Up until then we lived together at Bellevigne . . . my grandparents and my father and I.' He lifted his head, aroused by a thought. 'Our inheritance laws differ from yours in England. Everyone has a share in an estate, not just the eldest son.' His head dropped back. 'I was away most of the time at school, but returned here for the holidays. I suppose I must have missed having a mother, but it didn't seem to effect me much, there was always Grand'mère, and Zenobie, and Modestine over at the Home Farm. When I was sixteen, however, and my father forty-two, he came home one day and surprised us all with a bride, a girl twenty years his junior.'

In the ensuing pause Troy murmured: 'Isabeau,' and he nodded.

'Yes, Isabeau. I realise now that my father, though not a young man, was healthy and strong and he couldn't be expected to live his life out without a woman by his side. He had gone sixteen years and I suppose it was thought he would never marry again. You can imagine the shake-up it gave us all!' There was another silence and Lucien gave a short laugh. 'I'm told the middle teen years can be difficult—consider Philippe now! Certainly I was not an easy stepson for Isabeau. How could I be? She was only four years older than myself. When young Philippe came along, two years later, my father was delighted. At eighteen, I was less so, but away at university I chose to spend my vacations with friends and rarely visited Bellevigne. My grandfather, Valéry, died, and then my father was thrown from a horse and killed instantly. I was in England at the time, doing a stint of banking. I took over the family reins at the age of twenty-five.'

Troy said quietly: 'That must have been a difficult task for you to undertake.' She carefully placed her empty cup back on the tray. She could understand his arrogance a little more now. To take on the responsibilities of the de Sève estate, the Charon vineyards, a place in the Charon banks so young would demand strength. He had obviously succeeded in his task. The family would bring its problems. The old Comtesse, up in her wing, Isabeau, over-protective and probably bitter about her husband's untimely death, and Philippe, who obviously resented the authority of a mere brother.

Troy said suddenly: 'How did you know about my sculpture?'

Lucien smiled lazily. 'It's easy if you know the right people.'

'I'm sure it is,' agreed Troy dryly. 'You are a formidable person.' She swung her legs off the footstool and stood up, Lucien following suit. 'I can see that it would not do to get on the wrong side of you, Monsieur le Comte.'

They stood a pace away, their eyes held, Troy's slightly challenging, Lucien's enigmatic.

'I'm sure there will be no cause for that to happen,' Lucien remarked mildly, and matching his tone, Troy replied:

'I sincerely hope not. I wouldn't hold out much chance for my success. And now I really must go. I've taken up more of your time than I'm sure you can spare.'

He made no attempt to dissemble and she found herself liking his lack of flowery compliments.

'Today has been business, family business, which still must be discussed some time. Not now, I agree. I think you have had enough of de Sève history and affairs to last a lifetime.' He walked before her and opened the door. The young girl who served lunch was passing and he said: 'Tell André I want the car, Gabrielle.'

'*Oui*, Monsieur Lucien.' The girl gave Troy a friendly, curious glance and hurried on her way.

They followed more leisurely, Lucien giving a running commentary on various pieces of furniture, knowing Troy was interested, stopping when she admired a particularly fine corner chair set in a window alcove. Troy found him well versed in period history and when she enthused over an unusual pedestal table he said:

'You must come and delve at your leisure. I shall tell Jean-Jacques that you have my permission, and you can come and go, whether I am here or not.'

Troy turned her face to his, cheeks flushed with pleasure.

'You're very kind,' she stammered, and he waved a dismissive hand, opening another door leading out into the open. Once across a small terrace and down a flight of stone steps Troy stopped and looked back. She pointed to a stone shield.

'Is that your coat of arms, Lucien?' When he nodded she squinted up at it. 'It's a gauntlet, isn't it?' and then her eyes were caught by the words. '"*Il sait se défendre*" . . . "He can hold his own",' she translated thoughtfully, slanting him a glance. 'Hm, I imagine there's some truth there.'

He smiled. 'We are rather tenacious, I believe.'

'And the animals either side of the gauntlet?'

'The de Sève griffin,' supplied Lucien, his smile broadening. 'A fearsome beast, is he not? You'll find him all over the place, we're positively infested with the brute.' He indicated a low pillar gracing the balustrade. 'See, here he is, close to—a real hybrid monstrosity. Legend has it that he guards the de Sèves from ruin and slaughter . . . which is nice to know.'

'He *is* a mixture, isn't he?' Troy ran her fingers over the shape of the griffin. 'He has the body, legs and tail of a lion,' she peered round from all angles, 'and the head and claws of an eagle, with eagle's wings.'

'Don't forget the ears,' urged Lucien, eyes amused. 'I gather from the experts that they are extremely important.'

Troy reflected that the de Sève griffin and its master showed a distinctive predatory similarity and it would be an ill decision to do battle with either.

The Beaufighter drew up with a young man at the wheel. Lucien opened the door and Troy gained her seat gingerly. She expected him to say goodbye and had her smile and words of thanks ready on her lips when he surprised her by walking round and exchanging places with the young man.

Lucien said: '*Merci*, André,' and as the car moved slowly round the corner of the Château and out into the drive, Troy murmured in a troubled voice:

'André could have taken me.'

'So he could. When you know me better you will find that it is not necessary to concern yourself with my time. Why should I deny myself the pleasure of driving you? I have a position to uphold in the community—think what good it does my image to be seen in the company of a beautiful girl.' He gave her a lazy glance.

Cheeks aglow, Troy chuckled and shook her head. 'How ridiculous you are! It's much more likely to be the other way round,' and seeing him arch his brows in question, explained teasingly: 'The Beaufighter *and* a Count!' There, she had made him laugh. Amazing how rewarding even that was.

Lucien seemed indisposed to talk. Troy was not sorry. She needed a breathing space. She needed to analyse this strange sensation she felt each time he called her Victoire in that special way he had. So much had happened today that it was necessary to reflect. Certainly she felt in a strange mood after hearing the story of Valéry de Sève and her grandmother. It had touched her deeply. She was a true romantic and blessed with a strong imagination, both characteristics emotional ones.

And then there was Lucien de Sève, who was enough to throw anyone off balance. As he stopped the car to open the first field gate she watched him, the artist in her assessing his easy, relaxed walk, the neat symmetry of his physique. As a student of body form she was aware of what constituted a well-proportioned structure. As he walked back to the car she kidded herself that it was in a merely professional capacity that she liked to look at him, watch him move . . . and the sly little voice that insinuated otherwise was an idiot, an unrealistic idiot.

As they drove slowly down the road towards the farm Lucien commented:

'You're very quiet.'

Troy came out of her reverie with a start. He was watching the road ahead and his profile was sharply etched, brow, nose and jaw outlined against the afternoon sunshine, which seemed exaggerated against the air-conditioned interior of the Beaufighter.

Troy collected her wits. 'Sorry . . . I was thinking.'

He smiled and drew to a halt. 'Don't apologise.' He turned the key and the engine died. Moving slightly in the seat, he faced her. 'It's an agreeable surprise to find a female who doesn't chatter.'

'Ouch!' exclaimed Troy, half laughing, half annoyed. 'You are hard on us, aren't you? No wonder you've never found a wife, Monsieur le Comte! I'm beginning to think such a paragon could never exist!'

'I'm sure you're right, Victoire,' Lucien said equably. He put his hand into his inside jacket pocket and drew out an envelope. 'You remember I mentioned Grand'mère's ball? It is on the seventeenth, and Grand'mère extends an invitation to join us on that evening. I hope you find that you can accept.' He handed her the envelope.

Troy raised puzzled eyes to his face. 'It's very kind of Madame la Comtesse . . . but she doesn't know me . . . hasn't met me.'

'Grand'mère is a law unto herself. She has heard of you, of course, and quite rightly feels that it would be remiss to have a visitor staying at the Home Farm and not ask her along to join in the festivities.' He paused. 'Will you come?' He waited a moment and asked mockingly: 'You're not frightened of her, are you?'

'Certainly not!' protested Troy laughingly.

'Then why do you hesitate?'

She bit her lip and looked away, frowning slightly, her gaze following the flight of a bird as it darted in and out of the hedgerow searching for food.

'If the family are not to know about me, about the true reason for my being here, what will you tell them?' she asked, turning a curious face to him. Lucien said calmly:

'I shall tell them nothing. It's a policy of mine. It saves a lot of trouble in the long run.'

This brought forth a reluctant smile to her lips, but she persisted.

'But what will they think?'

He lifted his hands in an expressive gesture of dismissal, smiling cynically.

'A pointless exercise, Victoire, speculating upon another person's thoughts. Will you come?'

She turned the envelope in her hands. 'If I'm still here, I shall be glad to come, and shall write and inform Madame.' This was accepted with a brief: '*Bon*,' and then they left the Beaufighter and walked slowly across the yard to the farm. Pushing a truant strand of hair from her eyes, Troy looked up at him, squinting against the sun. She held out her hand.

'Goodbye, Lucien. Thank you for telling me about Grandmother. You've given me a lot to think about.'

He still clasped her hand as he said: 'I go to Bordeaux tomorrow, we have vineyards there also, and shall be away for a few days. Jean-Jacques will be on hand should you need anything. Do you think you could possibly try to keep out of trouble while I'm gone?' The grey eyes smiled lazily down at her.

An indignant protest, trembling on her lips, was replaced by a smile. 'I'll do my best,' she promised, and withdrew her hand. She entered the farmhouse and stood by the window, watching the distinctive cream car back into the side field and then disappear down the farm-road, Lucien's: '*À bientôt*, Victoire,' still in her ears.

See you soon . . .

She remembered the invitation and opened the envelope. The wording was formal, the de Sève crest at the top. She turned from the window and went up to her room, a thoughtful expression on her face. It was all very nice Lucien adopting a policy of saying nothing. She knew jolly well people would be curious and the logical assumption would be that it was Lucien who was inducing her to stay on. Did she mind having her name coupled with his?

She propped the invitation against the swivel mirror and nibbled her lip. Her spirits had plummeted and she knew why and it was laughable. To feel dismay because a man she hardly knew was going away for a few days!

In her well-ordered life it was not acceptable to be knocked off balance by a man so quickly. She had known it happen to others and had always been sceptical, distrusting such rapid emotional involvement. She distrusted still, but it made little difference. Her sense of reason seemed to have deserted her.

She lay back on the bed, her hands clasped behind her head, thinking what she had learned today. She felt confused, excited and apprehensive. A jumble of emotions, and all centred on Lucien de Sève.

Perhaps it was for the best that he was going away, it would give her a breathing space, thought Troy, and wondered whether it was possible to fall in love, totally unsuitably in love, after only three meetings.

CHAPTER FIVE

It was amazing how the sun shone every day and with such confidence. Looking at the pale blue sky with its white fluffy clouds, Troy supposed the Loiret to have rainfall, but to date she had not been caught in any. She was turning a gratifying tan, helped by wearing sun-tops and cool, sleeveless dresses. The injury to her thigh was much improved and the fresh air, the holiday mood and the good, wholesome food dished up by Modestine Marin suited her and brought an extra sparkle and vitality to her looks.

Troy wrote a long letter to Fiona, explaining what had happened since leaving Paris. She wondered what Fiona's reaction would be to the news that she had met, once again, the interesting ugly-attractive Frenchman, Fiona's own turn of phrase. As for the story of the wartime romance between Valéry de Sève and Victoria Courtland, Fiona had known Troy's grandmother well and would no doubt share Troy's own astonishment at what had happened in the rather awe-inspiring, so respectable old lady's past.

It was five days since Lucien de Sève had taken his leave. A breathing space of five long hot lazy days spent between the Home Farm and Bellevigne, graduating to a little gentle exploring of the village of Sève. At first, Jean-Jacques had ferried her to and fro, but then Troy found she was able to drive and soon André became used to having the red sports car under his expert care.

He was an engaging young man, André, and it was from him that Troy learned that most of the staff were descendants of families who had served the de Sèves for generations. He was courting the pretty little maid, Gabrielle, and they hoped to marry the following year, when Monsieur Lucien had promised them a house on the Estate.

Monsieur Lucien . . .

Five days without him in which Troy alternated between brisk pep-talks full of common sense, and daydreams which flustered and confused, throwing her into excited panic at the thought of his return.

Common sense won when she was away from the Château, but once at Bellevigne how could she stand back and take a cool assessment of her feelings when she was surrounded by people who never let her forget him for a minute? She found the staff friendly and helpful—Monsieur le Comte had left instructions that Mademoiselle Troy was to be welcomed and looked after, so welcomed and looked after Mademoiselle was. The Château itself was a constant reminder of the weight of Lucien's responsibilities. It was not extravagantly run, but the amount of staff needed so that it could be maintained efficiently was an eye-opener, and all of them depending upon him for a living.

Troy tried hard, never encouraging them to speak of him, but when they did, soaking in every word with concealed greediness. Bit by bit Lucien de Sève grew, and nothing she learned could diminish him. He was treated with loyalty, respect and deep affection, and even though she knew she was a fool to become involved in such a hopeless infatuation, she was powerless to stop the strengthening bond between them.

On this fifth day, the Château hummed with the

knowledge that Monsieur Lucien was due back from Bordeaux. It was purely accidental that the angle Troy had set her folding chair to gain a good view of the paddock and the black stallion, Sable, also allowed sight of the main drive along which the sleek, cream Beaufighter had to pass. Purely accidental, she told herself sternly, as she bent over her sketch pad.

When a shadow fell across the paper she thought that she had missed the car and her head came up eagerly. Disappointment was intense when she saw that it was Philippe and not Lucien. She hid her feelings and said pleasantly:

'*Bonjour*, Philippe,' and wondered why she was being honoured with his presence. She received a mumbled greeting and watched as he slouched to the paddock fence.

If the staff of Bellevigne had been friendly and welcoming, the family was less so. Isabeau was politely gracious whenever Troy saw her, which was not often. The old Comtesse, ensconced in her south wing, remained a recluse, and up till now Philippe had studiously ignored her. Now he had sought her out, on a Saturday, with no lessons to fill his time.

Troy carried on drawing, eyeing him out of the corner of her eye, feeling a rising exasperation. The boy had her sympathy, but really, with all his advantages, he ought to pull himself together. When he began to kick at one of the posts with the toe of his shoe, she said mildly:

'Philippe, you are disturbing my concentration and distracting the horse.'

Philippe gave a deep, bitter sigh, but he stopped kicking. Troy's pencil moved quickly over the page. Another quick glance at his sullen face decided her. Shock tactics sometimes worked.

'You know, Philippe, you're becoming a bit of a bore . . . a pain, in fact. I know you're fed up and unhappy, but the only person who can help you is yourself.' She turned over a page and began again, making more lightening sketches while Sable obliged by staying still, his tail swishing gently. She did not look at Philippe but was encouraged by him not walking off in a huff. 'Life's much easier mixing with happy people, and if you go around with an enormous chip on your shoulder and being grumpy then you must expect a lack of sympathy.'

He said stiffly: 'I beg your pardon. I did not know you disliked me so.'

'I don't dislike you. I just wish you'd organise yourself a bit better.'

'You do not understand,' he replied flatly.

'I understand you want to go to Orléans as a weekly boarder but that your mother is against the idea. Adults are always going on about when you're grown up, aren't they? and it's infuriating, but the fact remains that you're only fifteen and still have a few years to go until you're your own boss. Even then you can't always do what you want, but there's a better chance.'

'That's what Lucien says,' Philippe said grudgingly, coming closer.

'What you've got to do is come to terms with things. Life's too short to waste it by being miserable. Accept your brother's decision regarding Sable and the riding restrictions—I doubt either are to be for ever! Get your nose down to some work so that your tutor can praise—I gather you're quite clever so that shouldn't be difficult. And learn to smile a bit more.' She smiled herself, her eyes kind. 'You'd be surprised at the difference it makes! They'll be completely charmed by the new Philippe, and you might just find your folk more reasonable.'

'Maman would never let me go,' Philippe said.

'She might, if you get Lucien on your side.'

Philippe glanced at the sketch block and a note of surprise sounded in his voice. 'I say, they're good!'

'Thank you,' Troy replied dryly.

'I didn't know you could draw. You've captured Sable perfectly.' He paused and pointed a finger. 'Especially this one. Could I have it? I wish to put it on my wall.'

Troy was amused by the imperial request.

'I'm sorry, I need these, but if I have time I'll do one for you.' She waited for sulks, but he merely asked a little stiffly:

'Why do you need them?'

Turning the page again, Troy spoke as she worked. 'I have to choose something to sculpt, and Sable could become my choice. It's necessary that I know the way he looks from every angle, the way his body moves, so I draw him and take photographs and then work from both.' She selected a piece of charcoal and began a larger sketch. By gentle probing she learned a little more about the boy and realised that because most of the other boys his age who lived in the vicinity went to Bourges to the day school, Philippe felt an outsider. She tore off the sheet and held it out to him. 'Here's your picture of Sable, Philippe. Be careful, it smudges.'

Philippe exclaimed: 'Thank you—that's good. I wish I could draw, but I'm hopeless. If I could draw like that . . .' and his voice trailed.

Troy said briskly: 'There are other hobbies. What about photography? You could take photographs of Sable and the other horses, since they seem to be the only thing at the moment to interest you. You could even learn to develop and print. I have a camera you could borrow to try it out.'

'But I know nothing about photography.'

'Maybe not, but I do,' and seeing his look, Troy burst out laughing. 'My dear Philippe, do try to hide your doubts! Far from blowing my own trumpet, I merely tell you that we had to study photography at all levels at college.' She rose and began to pack up, thinking how easy it was to give other people advice. She was very conscious of the empty drive. What she ought to do was to go to the lawyer in Paris and deal with Grandmother's affairs through him instead of getting into a mess here!

They began to walk back towards the Château. Philippe observed thoughtfully:

'You're not a bit like I thought.'

Troy's brows rose. 'Oh?'

'You being a model. I didn't think you'd be able to draw or know about cameras and things,' he went on ingenuously.

'In other words you thought I was just an empty-head?' suggested Troy mildly, and Philippe went scarlet. She took pity on him. 'Don't worry, Philippe, I'm quite used to it, but you should never make judgements on outward appearance. For instance, you're not really a bore, are you?' and her eyes twinkled and Philippe grinned reluctantly. He said:

'Lucien and Grand'mère were talking the other day and Lucien said it didn't matter what you were like, it was enough just to look at you . . . and Lucien is a good judge.'

'Is he now?' managed Troy.

'I'll say! Lucien has an eye for horses and females. He never fails.' There was pride in Philippe's voice.

'Do you like your brother, Philippe?' Troy asked

tentatively, and he looked surprised.

'Gosh, yes, Lucien's all right . . . decent really . . . it's just that . . . oh, well, it's no use going on about it.'

'Not a bit,' agreed Troy cheerfully. 'I'll bring my camera tomorrow and we'll have a lesson on how to use it.' She glanced up at the house. 'Is Zenobie waiting for you, or me, do you think?'

They climbed the stone steps and Zenobie said: 'Your mother is looking for you, Philippe,' and he gave Troy a wry smile and went inside. Zenobie went on: 'Madame Claudine wishes you to take coffee with her, *mademoiselle*, if you would come this way.'

Oh no! thought Troy, unnerved, and begged to be allowed to wash the charcoal from her fingers. When that was done she hastily checked herself in the mirror. The navy and white striped dress was presentable, her hair was a little wild, she had washed it that morning—because it needed it, she had told herself, and not because a certain person was expected back from Bordeaux—and slicked it down with water, trying to tame it.

Zenobie gave her an encouraging smile and preceded her along the corridors and up flights of stairs so that Troy was soon lost.

As they entered the Comtesse's set of rooms Troy told herself sternly: The old lady can't eat you!

Claudine de Sève sat, straight-backed, in an elegant armchair with padded arms and buttoned upholstery of red and gold brocade. As Zenobie said: 'Mademoiselle Maitland, *madame*,' Troy moved forward to come beneath the sharp scrutiny of tiny button-bright eyes that travelled from her head to her toes and back again with intent regard.

'Good morning, Miss Maitland. How extremely good of you to visit me at such short notice,' Claudine de Sève said in excellent English. 'Thank you, Zenobie. Miss Maitland will pour.' Zenobie murmured: 'Very well, *madame*,' and gave Troy another supportive smile as she glided past. When the door closed behind her, Claudine de Sève gestured a hand towards the tray of coffee things.

Troy walked to the table and began to pour, asking the usual questions as to sugar and milk, carrying Madame's cup over to her and placing it within easy reach. She was amused, but careful not to show it. It could easily have been her own grandmother sitting with a critical eye waiting for her to make the tiniest mistake. Years of presiding at her grandmother's table gave one the utmost confidence in such matters, but Madame Claudine could not know that. Troy went back for her own cup and following another wave of the hand sat down on a similar chair opposite her hostess, who opened fire with all guns.

'You walk well, Miss Maitland, but I suppose that is part of your job.' She raised spectacles attached by a thin silver chain round her neck and peered through them. 'Is your hair naturally that colour, I wonder? It must be very difficult to manage . . . so thick and . . .' Madame paused to seek the word in English and resigned herself to one in French: '. . . *crépu*.'

Crépu, Troy knew, meant frizzy. *Bouclé* meant curly, a word Madame could have used to make sure of not offending. She was, Troy suspected, aware that her guest spoke French.

Troy remembered her manners and smiled. 'Your grandson tells me, *madame*, that you are soon to celebrate your eightieth birthday, and you have been kind enough to invite me to your ball. May I congratulate you? I hope that when I reach that great age my hair will look as beautiful as yours does now. As you suppose, mine brings its problems, but the colour is not one of them.'

Madame allowed the spectacles to drop, her gaze never wavering. After a moment the white, immaculately coiffured head inclined slightly at the compliment and she reached out a tiny hand to take her cup. Like everything else in the room the china was exquisite, fragile-thin and white, a fine gold rim its only decoration.

'You met my grandson at the Descartes', I understand,' Madame observed, dabbing her lips gently with a lace handkerchief. 'You know the Descartes well, Miss Maitland?'

'No, *madame* . . . I was merely a friend of one of their guests.'

'And now you find yourself on holiday, so conveniently close to Bellevigne, and my grandson.'

Troy said carefully: 'Coincidentally is a word I would rather use, *madame*.' She stared back at the accusing eyes and refused to be intimidated. She wished she could tell the old lady that she was no threat, that the reason her grandson was showing her attention was because of a wartime romance, but that story could not be retold here.

'Your leg is recovered?' Madame asked.

'Very nearly, *madame*. Dr Dubois will be removing the stitches on Monday.'

'Ah, *le bon docteur*! And will you then be savouring the further delights of our country?'

'I may stay a while in the Loiret, *madame*. It is a district unknown to me and one which appeals.'

This was received by a slight tightening of the lips and narrowing of the eyes. Dressed in black, relieved only by fine white lace at neck and cuffs, one hand resting on the top of an ebony cane, the other lying in her lap, Claudine de Sève looked every inch a Countess and a very formidable lady.

'You admire my room, Miss Maitland?'

'It is beautiful,' agreed Troy, her eyes wandering.

'You know something about period furniture?'

Troy gave a deprecating shrug. 'A little, *madame.*'

'You will appreciate, therefore, that we are surrounded by Louis Seize. I take a delight in keeping in the period, Miss Maitland. That secretaire over there is a fine example of Riesener.'

Troy followed her gaze. 'Indeed it is, *madame.*'

'And my little bureau. Is that not also a fine example?'

Had Troy been completely ignorant of eighteenth-century furniture she would still have had a prickling sensation at Madame's question. The tiny pixie face was bland and the button eyes slightly hidden by lowered lids, but there was something about the old lady that made Troy rise and study the bureau closer.

'I think you are teasing me, *madame,*' she said mildly, crossing her fingers and taking a chance. 'The bureau is, I think, Louis Quinze . . . sometimes called the Pompadour style, is it not?'

She could not tell whether Madame was pleased or annoyed at her bluff being called. She inclined her head and waved her stick imperiously for Troy to be re-seated.

'Not many English girls have heard of Riesener and fewer still could recognise one Louis reign from another,' Madame said, and Troy observed dryly:

'I doubt whether many French girls could either, *madame.* I studied furniture design at college and the eighteenth century particularly interests me,' and thank the Lord I had to do a special project on it too, thought Troy.

'I see. Have you been taken over to the Château, Miss Maitland?' Madame asked abruptly, and Troy smiled warmly.

'Yes, *madame*, and it is beautiful. You must be very proud of Bellevigne.'

'Do you, perhaps, see yourself as the future Comtesse de Sève?' The button eyes snapped and a faint colour tinged the powdered cheeks.

Troy carefully put down her empty cup before replying.

'Isn't that rather an odd question, *madame*? I have known your grandson only for a few days.'

The ebony stick cavorted and Madame's voice was harsh. 'Time means nothing! Within the first few minutes of meeting my husband I knew he was the man for me. If Lucien fancies you, he'll have you, but marriage is not in his mind. Has he made love to you?'

'You can hardly expect me to answer that question, *madame*.'

The old lady smiled grimly. 'If he hasn't, he will. A gorgeous thing like you—Lucien couldn't resist you! But he knows what is expected of him. An unknown English girl is not to be Comtesse de Sève!'

'Then you have nothing to worry about, *madame*,' urged Troy with studied calmness.

'He knows I dislike the English intensely . . .'

'*Madame*, you are mistaken if you think . . .'

'. . . and Juliette Descartes is being groomed for the role. A union with the Descartes is an admirable course of events. She would know what is expected of her and . . .'

'*Madame*, I beg you, do not upset yourself.'

'Lucien must marry within his own kind . . .' The angry tirade stopped and Troy rose to her feet, concerned. Madame's hand clawed at a small box on the nearby table and Troy hastened to open it for her, quickly handing over one of the tablets and waiting anxiously while the old lady's face became calmer.

'Shall I ring for Zenobie, *madame*?' she asked, and received a slight shake of the head. She sat down in her chair and waited, still perturbed.

At last Madame Claudine's colour improved and the button eyes, almost back to their original brightness, rested malevolently upon Troy. Madame said:

'My own fault. Dubois is always warning me to take life calmly. Calmly! How can I do that when there is so much to do and so little time to do it in!' Her lips pressed together. 'Don't fall in love with Lucien, girl. He'll only cause you heartbreak.'

The blood rushed to Troy's face. 'You are mistaken regarding your grandson. I am sure he has every intention of marrying a French girl, if he decides to marry at all. You need not concern yourself, *madame*,' she said quietly.

'I wish I could believe you. I have a tingling in my bones,' Madame replied sullenly, and briefly, Troy was reminded of Philippe. 'You have come here at the wrong time—I cannot pretend otherwise. Everything has been negotiated between the Descartes and myself. All that is necessary is for the announcement to be made. Lucien has merely been waiting for Juliette to finish her education.' She stared hard at Troy. 'I cannot like this modern view of life. A girl obeys first her parents and then her husband. You English are a bad influence.' Her hand lifted in a dismissive gesture. 'Ring for Zenobie, if you please, Miss Maitland. Thank you.' The stick stabbed the floor. 'Come, I wish you to have this.' The stick pointed to an exquisite cluster of porcelain flowers, no more than two inches in diameter, placed on the Pompadour bureau.

Troy stammered: 'But, *madame*, I couldn't possibly . . .'

'Of course you could, girl—take it.' It was the royal command. 'It is supposed to be Vincennes, but we cannot prove it. Go . . . take it.'

Troy could only obey. Refusing might bring on another attack. She was trying to convey her thanks, the flowers resting in the centre of her palm, when the door opened and Madame cut her short by saying firmly:

'Zenobie, Miss Maitland has finished her coffee. Thank you, Miss Maitland, for your company.' It was dismissal.

'Goodbye, *madame*. Thank you for your gift and for allowing me to see your beautiful room.' Troy followed Zenobie out, her thoughts and feelings in a jumble. Zenobie glanced at her face and smiled.

'You feel you have been through an ordeal, *mademoiselle*?'

Troy pulled a face. 'I do rather.'

'Madame has no time for people *sans caractère*,' stated Zenobie.

No time for the weak-kneed! Well, mine are shaking, thought Troy with grim amusement. A bleak feeling settled over her. A silly, stupid feeling, brought on entirely by her refusal to face facts. She asked: 'Has Monsieur Lucien returned?' The words were uttered before she realised she was thinking them.

'No *mademoiselle*. Jean-Jacques has just left for Paris with papers that need to be signed today. I understand that Mademoiselle Juliette has tickets for the ballet and Monsieur Lucien has made a detour to escort her.' They passed the hounds, César and Satan, who were lying across the doorway of the library. 'Those two will not rest contented until their master returns,'

Zenobie observed indulgently. 'You will stay to lunch, Mademoiselle Troy?'

'No, thank you, Zenobie,' and Troy softened the refusal with a smile. Zenobie looked uncertain but said nothing, watching as Troy collected her sketch-block and satchel. Walking out to the car, she received a cheery wave from André and as she drove down the drive she remembered how eagerly she had waited earlier for the Beaufighter to appear.

Juliette Descartes. As Madame Claudine said, a most suitable liaison, and Troy wondered whether Lucien would end up obliging his grandmother. Juliette was young and pretty and Lucien was obviously extremely fond of her . . .

Stop this! she told herself firmly. The Beaufighter was probably already nosing its way into Paris and Lucien was escorting Juliette to the ballet tonight. Remember that, Troy Maitland!

The following morning the first thing she saw was the china flowers. Highlighted by a shaft of sunlight, they sat, delicately beautiful, on Madame Marin's highly polished chest of drawers. Troy had not slept particularly well and the flower-cluster vividly brought back Madame Claudine's angry interview. She wiped the worried look off her face as Modestine brought in the breakfast tray, a service she insisted on performing every morning, and refusing to pander to the Comtesse's wild theories any more Troy set to and tackled breakfast, surprised to find how hungry she was.

She had hardly begun before Modestine was back, consumed with an air of urgency.

'Mademoiselle Troy, you must come quickly to the telephone. Monsieur le Comte wishes to speak with you.' She picked up Troy's silk dressing-gown and held it out for her.

Troy stared in mounting exasperation, not helped by a surge of panic.

'But, Modestine, my egg will get cold,' she protested weakly, seeing no softening in her landlady's expression. 'Couldn't you say I'd ring him back?'

Modestine was shocked. '*Mais non*, Mademoiselle Troy! Hurry, we must not keep Monsieur waiting.'

'No, we mustn't do that,' grumbled Troy irreverently under her breath, and slipping her feet into mules and her arms into the dressing-gown she allowed herself to be hustled down the stairs.

'*Bonjour*, Monsieur le Comte.'

'You are extremely formal, Victoire, this morning.' The voice at the other end of the telephone was just as she remembered it.

'How can I be otherwise, when for five days your title has been on everyone's lips?' she replied coolly, ignoring the leaping of her senses as she heard him laughing softly.

'But I do not wish to hear it on yours . . . and five days! Is it really five days, Victoire?' The familiar teasing note was back in his voice.

Troy ground her teeth, brain working madly. Did he think she had counted the days? 'I believe so . . . yes, it must be, as Dr Dubois is removing my stitches tomorrow.'

'Ah, yes, and how is your injury—are you recovered? Have you had any more adventures while I've been away?'

I had a particularly formidable one yesterday, thought Troy broodingly, but said: 'I'm much better, thank you, and I'm not normally accident-prone—perhaps it's something to do with you?'

He laughed. 'It might be, at that. I'm pleased to

hear you are improved. I shall call for you in under the hour and we shall inspect the remains of the cottage and . . .'

'I'm sorry,' said Troy, who was not sorry at all, 'but I can't this morning.'

There was the fraction of a pause. 'I see.'

The bloody arrogance of the man! raged Troy. He's been gone five days—and damn him, of course he knows I've counted them—and returns blithely expecting me to be waiting and available.

'You are, perhaps, free after lunch?'

'Yes.'

'*Bon!* I shall pick you up at two o'clock. *A tout à l'heure!*'

Troy walked slowly back to her room and eyed the cold egg distastefully. The coffee was still hot in the pot, however, and she drank it down gratefully—nerves had dried up her throat. Which was ridiculous. Why should Lucien de Sève make her nervous, for goodness' sake! She would see him this afternoon purely on business matters. She would be on guard, no more allowing the way he said Victoire to undermine her resolve either. Let him do his philandering in Paris. At the ballet. With Juliette Descartes.

She chose one of her prettiest dresses to wear—and why not? she argued with that sly other-self that mocked, why not? It was a hot day and the dress a cool one, did it matter that the buttermilk colour complemented her tanned skin and flaming hair, or the deep square neck and flared skirt showed off her figure? Her hair she brushed until it bristled and her face she finger-tipped with sun-cream. A generous helping of perfume in the right places and a touch of coral lipstick and she was done. She collected her camera and paused briefly at the mirror.

A slow deep smile parted her lips. No harm in looking and feeling one's best, even for a business meeting, she told the girl in the mirror. With a toss of hair, a tilt of hip, she swung away and ran lightly down the stairs.

Troy and Philippe spent all the morning with the camera. The time passed so quickly that both were surprised when they were informed that lunch was served. They walked leisurely back from the paddock where Philippe had been putting theory into practice, still discussing the principles involved, and Troy, watching the boy's animated face, thought that the bug had bitten.

'You will, of course, stay to lunch,' said Philippe, sounding very much like his brother. Troy felt a quickening of the pulse as they entered the Salle Ovale. Lucien was pouring wine. No change, then, she told herself helplessly, as she allowed herself to be seated at the oval table, having made her greetings to Isabeau, Jean-Jacques and finally, Lucien, who was regarding her with slight amusement on his lean, sardonic face. Almost, Troy thought crossly, after that first upward glance, as if he knows what's going on inside my head—which he can't possibly! Throughout lunch she barely spoke two sentences to him, studiously avoiding catching his eye. Tiresomely juvenile, as she afterwards admitted to herself.

It was not to be expected that Philippe would change instantly from an angry young man into one of sunshine and laughter, but he joined in the general conversation quite amiably and when asked, proved voluble on the morning's instruction. As soon as he was able, Philippe escaped, Troy's camera slung round his neck. When the door closed behind him, Lucien remarked:

'You must have magic powers, Victoire. Will it last, do you think? My eternal thanks, if it does. We shall cross our fingers and pray, eh, Isabeau, that photography eclipses the urge to ride Sable!' Having toasted Troy with his glass, forcing her to meet his eyes, he then turned his head to smile at Isabeau.

Isabeau returned the smile and murmured something appropriate. For the rest of the meal Troy was trying to work out why Isabeau was not pleased. There had been something in her eyes, some quick flash of .. coldness? . . . resentment? that Troy found disturbing. Surely she was not jealous of Troy's friendship with Philippe?

André's eyes looked on with approval as he brought the Beaufighter round from the garage and opened the door for Troy to get in. If Lucien noticed the look and the subsequent flush on Troy's cheeks, he made no comment, but as the Beaufighter eased its way out of the park Troy felt compelled to ask:

'Is the reason for my being here still a secret?' and when Lucien answered with a nod of the head, she went on: 'Where have you said we're going this afternoon?'

Lucien gave a lift of his dark brows. 'My dear girl, there's no necessity to say anything. Many moons ago I realised the less people know the easier life becomes.'

It doesn't stop people speculating, thought Troy, remembering Madame Claudine's accusations and André's look, and there had been an odd little silence after lunch when Lucien had glanced at his watch and asked Troy if she had finished as he had ordered the Beaufighter for two o'clock.

'If you think that anything you do passes unnoticed you must be singularly obtuse—and that you certainly are not!' retorted Troy, and he threw back his head and laughed.

'Poor Victoire! I'm so used to Bellevigne that I'm immune to the feudal atmosphere. Has it been getting you down?' He slanted her a glance. 'I gather you had the royal summons yesterday. I had hoped to be with you when that occurred. How did you get on with Grand'mère? She can be a battleaxe sometimes.'

'I found her amazingly like my own grandmother,' confessed Troy, relieved to find that Madame Claudine had said nothing of her outburst.

'*Mon Dieu!* I didn't think there could be two in the same mould!'

Troy chuckled and then became serious. 'Lucien, your grandmother gave me a gift yesterday and I'm not sure I should keep it. She insisted that I should have a lovely porcelain flower cluster. It must be awfully valuable.'

Lucien frowned and shot her a sharp look. 'Oh, hell! Grand'mère must have been damnably rude to you—I'm sorry. She does that, insults someone and then gives them a present to make up.' He flicked her another shrewd glance. 'She's not done that for a long time—I wonder what she said to you?' When Troy remained silent, only her heightened colour betraying that there might be some truth in his speculation, he went on: 'Hm . . . you're not going to tell, evidently. Well, we'll leave that for the time being . . . and yes, you're to keep the thing, it might make Grand'mère hold her tongue in future.'

Troy shifted uneasily in her seat. He sounded philosophical, but something told her he was keeping his true feelings in check. There was a set look to his face that worried her, and the thought that she might be the cause of trouble between Lucien and Madame Claudine gave her some concern. She asked quickly:

'Can we reach the cottage by road?' to change the subject.

Lucien shook his head. 'Not completely . . . and here is where we park.' So saying, he pulled off the road on to the grass verge. They left the car and walked through a gateway along a track bordered by rows and rows of waist-high vines. Lucien pointed to a helicopter hovering over the Estate further south.

'We're having the vine sprayed against pest and disease. It's a good day for it, very little wind.' He paused and bent to examine a nearby plant, his hands parting the leaves with professional confidence. As they continued to walk, his eyes covered the vines with critical intensity, talking as he did so. 'We're into the second half of the crop's year, it starts in the autumn, after the vines are stripped of the grape.' He glanced at her, saying positively: 'You'd like that, it's a glorious sight, all red and gold.'

'What happens then?' asked Troy, curious, liking to hear him discourse on a subject he obviously knew inside out.

'The shoots are trimmed and pruned and nursed through the winter and by the middle of March the sap begins to rise and then we have to be careful of late frost. We climb this stile, can you manage? Yes, of course you can. Those long legs of yours can tackle anything!'

This observation inhibited Troy slightly, but she managed the stile in comparative modesty and Lucien followed, swinging himself over easily. Their path now lay through a wood, the undergrowth hard and dry beneath their feet, the trees thickening as they progressed deeper.

'You've just got the vines through the late frosts,' prompted Troy, who did not like to leave things half finished. She was interested, anyway, and it seemed a safe subject to talk about. She also had the excuse to look at him if he kept on, and that gave her satisfaction too. She was still trying very hard to treat the afternoon as a business meeting, but was helplessly aware that her resolve was slowly, but steadily, crumbling. The touch of his hand on her arm as he helped her over the stile cracked the already weakened structure and now, whenever she could, she feasted her eyes on him, giving in to the inevitable. Somehow, whatever Lucien wore seemed right. He had the happy knack of being totally at ease in the clothes of the moment. This afternoon he was casually dressed in light-weight grey pants and a short-sleeved open-neck shirt. He looked tanned and fit and without a trouble in the world. At her prompting he turned his head and regarded her steadily for a moment and, satisfied that she was not being merely polite, replied:

'Then comes the all-important flowering in June and we pray for settled warm weather. In July the grapes begin to appear in tiny clusters and by the end of August they're full grown and ripening nicely. There's comparative calm until September when the most crucial decision for every *vigneron* arrives—when to pick the grape. Careful!' Lucien grabbed hold of her as she stumbled on the rutted earth. 'Do you intend to sprain an ankle next?' he asked teasingly.

Although they were brief, Troy was very conscious of those few seconds of contact. She covered up with a laughing exclamation:

'Don't tempt fate, please!' and swung her eyes to the ground. It was better if she did not look at him. 'Go on . . . what do you do when the date is decided?'

'Life becomes extremely serious,' Lucien told her promptly. 'Once we start we are committed for three weeks. We have the same families come to us year after year for the picking, often comprising three generations, plus everyone who can be spared from Bellevigne.'

'And Monsieur le Comte? Does he join in?' Troy asked teasingly, and he replied with mock severity:

'Of course! It is the custom for the head of the house to pick the first grape, but I have to confess that other commitments have claim to my attention. For the pickers, it is heads down, backs breaking, starting in the cold mists of early morning and going on until sunset. At the end, however, we have a good feast and sample a few glasses of wine!' He touched her arm and stopped. 'There is the cottage, or rather, what remains of it.'

Troy peered through the trees and saw a clearing in the centre of which stood the ruins of a small house. In silence they walked up to it, and Troy felt disappointment spreading over her. Even though Lucien had warned her, she had been hoping that in some way the house could be made habitable, but now she saw that this was not possible. She picked her way carefully through nettles, long grass and brambles, circling the shell, finally joining Lucien who stood watching her.

'You are disappointed,' he stated at last, and Troy gave him a quick, selfconscious smile and shrugged.

'It's a pity,' she said.

'What would you have done with it, had it been habitable?'

She turned her head in surprise, eyes wide. 'Why, turn it into a studio, of course!'

Lucien nodded slowly. 'A studio . . . *naturellement*.'

Troy glanced at the ruin and asked curiously: 'Do you think our grandparents met here?'

'It is possible.' He was amused at her romanticism.

'You are thinking of a trysting place? But, *mignonne*, there was no one to oppose their love for each other, no need for secrecy . . . but it is possible that they met here.'

Mignonne! It did not mean anything, was merely a term of affection, but how thankful she was that her face was turned from him at that moment. She went on stubbornly: 'I'm sure they met here,' and shivered suddenly.

'You are cold?' Lucien asked, concerned, and Troy smiled uneasily and shook her head.

'Ghosts, I think.'

'Let us go. There is something I want to talk about, to show you, in fact, and although I scoff at your ghosts this place always saddens me. Now that it is so overgrown and the trees have encroached, the sun never reaches it.'

Some way along the track Troy looked back. Poor Valéry and Victoria . . . tossed apart by the fragments of a war.

'Victoire! *Allons donc!*'

Lucien's voice, calling her to hurry, broke the spell, scattered the ghosts. She turned and hurried towards him and allowed him to help her over the stile, glad to feel the sunlight on her face once more.

CHAPTER SIX

As the Beaufighter sped smoothly along the winding lanes, Troy said thoughtfully:

'If the cottage has been a ruin for all these years why has Grandmother received an income from it?'

Lucien replied patiently: 'The cottage and the land merely provide sanction in legal terms. So far as you are concerned, as her beneficiary, the Estate will continue these payments. However, if you wish, you could sell your claim back to the Estate and the lump sum can be invested—but you would need to seek advice on that.' He swung through the gateway and into Bellevigne park. 'There is no necessity to make a hasty decision.' He gave her a fleeting glance. 'I have a proposition to put to you.'

'Oh?' said Troy guardedly, and his lips twitched.

'*Mais oui* . . . a most proper one, I assure you.' He negotiated the fountain and pulled up outside the office wing. André, his head inside Isabeau's car, working on the engine, looked their way, ready to be on call. Lucien killed the engine and swivelled in his seat to look at her appraisingly. 'If I could offer you the use of a studio, would you stay on for a while?'

Troy stared at him in astonishment. 'I don't understand. A studio? Where?'

'Here, right under your nose.' He opened the window and called André, who abandoned his job and came over. 'André, will you fetch the keys to the store rooms, please?'

'A proper studio?' prompted Troy, her feelings in a whirl, eyes wide and intent upon every expression on his face, each nuance in his voice.

'Yes, a real studio. When the new stables were built some years ago we converted the old stable block here into space for the cars. The loft above was used as store rooms, but part of the area, in Grandfather's latter life, was converted into a studio. He painted in his spare time and as no one else had either his talent or his interest, the studio after his death became another store room. It wouldn't take long to clear and clean up the place . . . *et voilà* . . . your studio!'

Troy put fingertips to forehead and said helplessly: 'That sounds terrific, but I couldn't possibly. I couldn't.'

'Why not?'

'Because . . . oh, because it would be too much of an imposition.'

'Tell me, Victoire, had the cottage been habitable would you have made it into a studio?'

'Well, yes, but . . .'

'There is your answer. We cannot provide a habitable cottage, but we can provide a studio here at the Château. One, moreover, that is being wasted. You also need time to consider your inheritance. It seems perfectly straightforward to me.'

'You make it sound like that, but it isn't,' Troy protested.

'There's someone in England who would not approve?'

'No! I'm free of all commitments in England,' she told him impatiently. 'I'm not thinking of my side of it . . . what about your grandmother? How is Madame Claudine going to like me using her husband's studio?'

'Grand'mère is not a sentimentalist. I shall talk to her.'

'Just like that? Monsieur le Comte wishes it?'

'Power is useful if it isn't abused,' Lucien replied calmly.

'But what will people think?' The colour rushed to her face beneath his ironical look. He waited before answering, taking the keys from André, the young man giving Troy a shy smile before leaving them.

'Why should they think anything?' asked Lucien. He pushed open the door and got out, walking round to open the passenger door. 'I am a realist. I suspect that you are a very determined young lady, Victoire Maitland, and that ultimately you will accept my offer because it is too good to refuse. I predict that in one week you will be working in the studio and will have forgotten all the arguments trembling on your lips at this moment. They are as nothing compared to your work.'

Troy regarded him gravely. He was an astute man. To work, really work, in such glorious surroundings was an opportunity she would be an idiot to turn down. She made up her mind quickly before having second thoughts, saying abruptly:

'Very well, thank you, if Madame permits, I accept your offer.'

'*Bon*. Valéry would have liked the idea of his studio being used again.' Lucien led the way across the courtyard and climbed the stairs on the outside wall, unlocking the door at the top and guiding Troy through a storage room, unlocking another door at the far end. He stood aside for her to enter.

'You will have to use your imagination a little,' he claimed, following her in, 'but when the windows are cleaned the light is good, the walls need a coat of paint but are basically sound. There's a sink . . .'

'With running water? Oh, good!' exclaimed Troy, her eyes travelling round, assessing the place. She began to feel excited. 'This would do splendidly,' she murmured, her mind already planning where her things would go. 'In fact, it's perfect.'

Lucien watched her, a half-smile on his lips. He brought out a pocket-book and pen and asked: 'What will you need?'

Troy swung round, thinking hard. 'A good strong work bench . . . perhaps a couple more shelves, and do you think we could put in a heavy-duty sludge trap in the sink, for blockages?' She stopped, feeling a surge of uneasiness rushing through her, her eyes fixed on his bent head as he wrote in the notebook. 'Lucien . . . why are you doing this?'

He looked up. 'Does there have to be a reason . . .' he paused and a brow quirked, '. . . other than those I've already given?'

Troy dropped her gaze. 'No, I suppose not.' She absently rubbed a finger to her forehead, smoothing away the tiny frown that had appeared. 'I shall need polythene sheeting and three plastic bins with airtight lids for the clay. A modelling stand, two, if possible, but if you know a carpenter I can draw what I want, it wouldn't take much to knock together. As for my tools, it's ridiculous to get more when my own are sitting over in England. In any case, I'm used to them, they're old friends. I suppose I could go back for them . . .' and she lifted her eyes once more, questioningly.

Lucien thought for a moment. 'No, there's no need. Have you someone who can pack them up for you?'

'Yes, Fiona, we share the house, but there's quite a list.' She began to tick the items from her fingers, eyes dancing. 'Hammer, saw, screwdriver, hacksaw, pliers, wire cutters, knives, scissors, chisel and mallet, not to mention screws, nails, nuts and bolts.' She pulled a comical face. 'Not a very ladylike occupation, is it?'

Lucien looked amused. 'I do know a little about the technique of sculpture and quite understand that you need a framework—I've forgotten the term used, though.'

'Armature,' supplied Tory. 'I assume I can get clay locally?'

'I'll make enquiries.' The book was opened again and a note made. 'All you have to do is to telephone your friend Fiona, give her the list and I'll contact someone who'll collect the case—can they all be packed into a suitcase?—and bring it over on the ferry. I have a cousin, a wine shipper, who's always crossing the Channel.'

'Do you think he could manage two suitcases?' asked Troy hopefully, adding: 'Clothes . . . I shall need a few more if I'm to stay on longer.'

'I'm sure he could.' Lucien perched on a packing case and watched her prowl among the boxes, old furniture, rolls of carpeting, coming to a halt at an upright piano.

'What medium did your grandfather use, do you know, Lucien?' Troy lifted the lid and touched the keys gently. It sounded tinny and out of tune.

'Watercolours, mostly, but there's one of the Château done in oils in Grand'mère's room.'

Troy frowned across at him and said with great firmness: 'I don't think we should do anything until you ask Madame Claudine.'

Lucien regarded her indolently, hooded eyes faintly amused. 'Very well,' he said.

I won't get too excited, Troy was thinking, just in case she puts her foot down.

'What's the matter? Ghosts again?' His voice was

teasing and Troy smiled ruefully and put down the lid, walking back slowly.

'They'll only be friendly ones, won't they?' she observed lightly, and came to a halt in front of him. Something in the way he was considering her brought a hint of colour to her cheeks and she wanted to look away but could not.

'Are you like your grandmother?' Lucien asked, and Troy, oddly at a loss, replied:

'They say I am. Why?'

'Don't you think we should feel an affinity, we two? I am supposed to be very much like Valéry, even bear his name, and you are like your grandmother, and another Victoire.' Unhurriedly he straightened and reaching out, touched her hair. 'She must have been a beautiful woman, your grandmother.'

Her heart turned a silly somersault in her breast. His fingers raked through her hair and cupped the back of her neck. Troy made a token gesture of protest, her hands fluttering against his chest as he drew her near, discovering she had lost all power of speech. As his lips touched hers each sensible thought went out of her head and she was consumed with only a sense of touch and a feeling of exquisite sweetness rushing through her.

'Why did you do that?' Troy asked at long last, her voice husky. It was a banal question, but the best she could do at that particular moment. Their first kiss on the Descartes' balcony had been child's play to this. She felt as though if Lucien were not there to support her she must surely fall. No one should have that much effect on a person, she thought wildly, it simply was not fair! Striving for composure, she lifted her eyes to his and found them gazing down at her quizzically. Damn him, surely he realised she did not expect an answer to her ridiculous question? For the life of her she could not think of a single sensible thing to say. She was now fitted more snugly into his body as his hands left her hair and moved leisurely down her back, one thumb running impudently down her spine, making her arch herself more closely, while the other hand supported her weight with ease.

He smiled crookedly and said mildly: 'Why? It seemed a good idea at the time . . . you could call it a sort of experiment.'

'I see,' replied Troy breathlessly, unable to meet his eyes any longer and very much aware of their bodily contact and of his warm breath on her face. Was the strong, steady beat of his heart, pressed against the palm of her hand, more rapid than usual? Certainly her own was thumping away like mad. If only she could redeem herself by at least making a token struggle to get away, but her limbs could have belonged to someone else, and in any case, she did not want to escape. She was exactly where she wanted to be. At least she had the sense to play it light.

'A sort of reincarnation experiment, you mean?'

'Exactly!' The wicked grey eyes slanted down at her and he looked foxier than ever. 'Reluctantly, however, the research into this fascinating subject will have to cease for the moment. I can see Jean-Jacques coming across the yard with purpose in his step. I'm obviously required,' and he slowly released her.

'Saved by Jean-Jacques,' Troy responded flippantly, glad to sink down on to the packing case and make the strap of her sandal the excuse to hide her face. She heard Lucien walk through the other store room and open the outer door, heard the sound of their conversation, but not their words, and by the time Lucien returned she was standing by the window, her fingers rubbing the dust from the pane leaving a round circle of bright sunlight.

He said: 'Sorry, I have to go, something's cropped up that needs my attention. When shall you telephone your friend Fiona?'

'In the early evening, I think, would be best.'

'I'll tell Jean-Jacques to expect you and he'll help you to get through. Here are the keys . . . you don't have to rush away. If you think of anything else you'll need, just let Jean-Jacques know.' He tossed her the keys and she caught them. Just as he was nearly out of the door, she said:

'Lucien.' He stopped and turned slowly, face showing that his thoughts were already flying ahead to whatever problem he was about to deal with. She could be as detached and clinical as he. 'Lucien, if I agree to this studio it is on the clear understanding that you remember who you are. You are *not* your grandfather and *I* am not my grandmother. There will be no seduction scenes, Lucien de Sève, in the guise of experiments or otherwise!'

His face changed to horrified amazement. '*Mon Dieu!* That would be taking experimentation too far,' he protested, those comical eyebrows high above dancing eyes.

Troy bit her lip, glaring at him frustratedly. Honestly, he was the limit! What chance did she have when he looked like that, teasing and challenging at the same time? She was hopeless at these kind of games. She would have to make him understand.

'I mean it, Lucien. I shall be here to work.'

Lucien shrugged expressively. '*Naturellement*, Victoire . . . while I prefer to play my seduction scenes without anyone breathing over my shoulder—ghosts or otherwise,' and on that sardonic observation he viewed her calmly, and when finally satisfied that their conversation was over, inclined his head courteously and made his getaway.

Lucien telephoned Troy later at the Home Farm. He had on his brisk, business voice.

'Victoire? Jean-Jacques has booked a call to England for seven o'clock. Grand'mère has agreed the use of the studio and Zenobie is preparing a room for your stay . . .'

'Lucien—wait! I can't stay at the Château!'

'Why not? We have enough room. It will be more convenient.'

'You do steamroller a person, don't you? Perhaps I don't *want* to stay at the Château.'

He laughed softly. 'Oh, but I know you better than you think. You will adore to stay at Bellevigne.' His voice changed and became encouraging. 'Come, agree that my suggestion makes sense. I have already spoken to Modestine . . .'

'But, Lucien . . .'

'Perhaps the thought of seeing more of Jean-Jacques can tempt you?'

Troy took a deep breath. 'Jean-Jacques is intelligent, charming and polite . . .'

'*Mais oui*, why else do I employ him?'

'. . . and he doesn't make me lose my temper!'

'How boring, Victoire! Start packing.' There was a click and he was gone. Troy replaced the telephone and found a silly grin on her face which she hastily got rid of and went to do as she was told.

Apart from being intelligent, charming and polite, Jean-Jacques was also efficient and tactful. When Fiona's voice came through from England on the telephone he unobtrusively left the office.

'Fiona, it's Troy.'

'Troy! How are you? I got your letter and still can't believe all you wrote. You've saved me writing back, but I'm damned if I can remember all the do's and don'ts, especially the don'ts that I was going to put in it! I doubt you'd have heeded them, anyway.'

'I don't suppose I would have,' agreed Troy, laughing a little. 'Fiona, listen, have you a paper and pencil handy? Take this down—I'll explain in a minute.' Troy read out her list of requirements and when she finished went on to the explanations. There was silence at the other end and then Fiona gave an audible sigh.

'It's getting a bit complicated, Troy, isn't it? I mean, I hope you know what you're doing—you're so bloody naïve at times. But you're in too deep, aren't you, to back out?'

' 'Fraid so.' Troy's eyes wandered round the office. Lucien's presence dominated the room even when he was not there. She added staunchly: 'I haven't completely gone under yet, though.'

'You will. I knew that man was dynamite the minute I saw him looking at you. At a guess I'd say the guy usually gets what he wants. Just make sure it's what you want too.' Fiona tactfully changed the subject and passed on news from her end. She mentioned a new outfit she had just bought and Troy interrupted to say quickly:

'I nearly forgot ... Fiona, will you pack a case of clothes for me? I leave it to you what to put in, except include my riding gear and a few decent evening dresses, especially the red.'

Fiona exclaimed: 'Wow! The Calvin Klein?'

'Uh-huh ... I've decided the old Comtesse's birthday is just the occasion for it.'

Fiona said worriedly: 'Troy, are you sure you're

doing the right thing by staying? I know the studio is an incentive, but . . .'

'Of course I'm not sure, but I'd kick myself afterwards if I didn't,' acknowledged Troy.

'Ah, well, *che sera, sera,* as Doris Day used to warble, and which they tell me translates into the well-known adage, what will be, will be. Pearls of wisdom drop daintily from my lips for all ocasions.'

Troy laughed. 'Your accent is terrible, Fiona, and another pearl you can store away is *qui ne risque rien n'a rien,* which means, who risks nothing has nothing!'

'How apt. Have they anything about making one's bed and lying on it? Don't answer that! They're sure to. Just you keep your mind off the Count and on the work.'

'I'll try,' promised Troy, smiling into the telephone.

Troy was to have personal experience of Lucien's capacity for getting things done during the next few days. Men appeared to clear and paint the studio, the wiring and heating was overhauled and a work-bench and modelling stands delivered within three days. Clay and plaster-of-Paris arrived, as did the two suitcases from London, and as Lucien had predicted, Troy was working in the studio one week later. But he was wrong about the doubts. They still came.

Mostly when she looked out of the window and caught sight of the familiar dark head and suited form sliding behind the wheel of the Beaufighter, or running up the steps into the Château.

She was royally housed in a guest suite in the east wing, consisting of a bedroom, sitting room and bathroom. The staff barely concealed their approval of her visit, which caused Troy a fair amount of inner embarrassment and made her spend more time in the studio than perhaps she would have done. They became used to her odd hours of working and young Gabrielle would often bring a tray over, hoping to catch sight of André and linger to have a hasty few minutes with him. How simple their love for each other was, thought Troy enviously, encouraging the meetings all she could.

She saw more of Philippe than anyone. A firm friendship had grown between them and he would climb the stairs to the studio and make coffee and they would talk photography. Philippe was now the proud possessor of his own camera and Lucien had promised a fully equipped darkroom if his enthusiasm stood the test of time . . . precipitated by an encouraging report from Philippe's tutor.

The studio became less bare. The piano had been left in the corner, but was now joined by an armchair and sofa, a table of the gate-legged type and cups and a coffee percolator. Philippe produced a record player, a set of classical records because Troy happened to mention that she liked to work to music, and endless photographs for her to look through and criticise.

She saw very little of Isabeau, but the few times they met Troy was unable to penetrate her polite reserve, and of Madame Claudine she saw nothing. This did not mean that Madame was unaware of what was going on, however, another reason for keeping out of Lucien's way.

In this she did not have to try very hard. Lucien was away more than he was at the Château and would come and go without warning. Philippe's early morning rides had been reinstated and Troy had taken to joining him, mounted on a brown mare named Cléo. On the odd occasion, Lucien went with them, and the ride was always heightened in the degree of pleasure for Troy. Since that first day in the studio he had made no attempt to touch her, which should have relieved her but did not, and the fact that it did not barely surprised her. She was becoming philosophical about her feelings for Lucien de Sève, although her resolve to keep them in check was not impaired.

Coming back from one of the morning rides, Troy and Philippe were walking away from the stables, both more than ready for their breakfast, when Philippe said suddenly:

'There's the Beaufighter. André's back from the airport.'

Troy followed his gaze and saw the car draw slowly to a halt in the courtyard.

'Has Lucien gone somewhere?' she asked, the day beginning to stretch out endlessly before her. Philippe nodded, and said:

'Yes, Italy, didn't you know?' He waved to André, who came towards them. They exchanged greetings and when Philippe ran into the Château to change, André handed Troy an envelope, saying:

'From Monsieur Lucien, *mademoiselle.*'

'Thank you, André,' Troy replied, pretending an indifference she did not feel. She was conscious of his barely concealed look of approval as she took the letter into the studio to read. She still felt an outsider in the Château, but in the studio, with its familiar smells and objects, she was able to completely relax. Once inside she studied the envelope. Lucien's handwriting was like himself, neat and well formed, the letters joining and flowing, showing strength in the strong downward strokes and sensitivity in the general artistic forming of the overall effect. Only the word 'Victoire' was on the envelope and wonderingly, she opened it up. The letter was businesslike and to the point.

'"Victoire, I have been in touch with Sir John Daviot in London, explaining the situation here, and he agrees with me that you should continue your weekly studies, if possible. He suggested Honoré d'Arcy. Despite being highly recommended by Daviot I have made enquiries and I find d'Arcy has a sound reputation. There is, therefore, a place in his teaching class every Thursday for you. André knows the studio address in Paris and will take you. I hope my 'steam-rollering' will not send you into a temper! I return from Italy in time, I hope, for Grand'mère's party—and so, until then, Lucien de Sève."'

Tomorrow was Thursday. In a daze Troy read the letter again. Honoré d'Arcy! She had no need to look up his credentials, his name being well known to her, she had even been to an exhibition recently in London where certain pieces of his work had been on display.

She sat down, trying to get her thoughts in order. Why had Lucien done this? Did he realise just what a tremendous experience this weekly class would be for her? How like him to arrange it all and then fly off to Italy without giving her a chance to discuss it with him. Could she accept this generous offer? She already felt deeply in his debt with the use of the studio.

She rose restlessly and began to walk round the studio, a slight frown on her face. Was it purely altruistic reasons that made him so generous, or were his motives more complex? He was a business man and used to summing up situations to his best advantage. She shied away from thinking such cynical thoughts, but they had to be faced. Her inheritance from Bellevigne was the reason for her being here and because Lucien had not pressed her, she had put the decision of what to do with it to the back of her mind.

Looking at it from the de Sève point of view, if she sold out then the whole thing could be forgotten. And then there was this . . . this attraction between them. It was there, they both knew it was there. Was he being kind to her to undermine her defences? Awful thought! How could she even begin to think like that? Yet she could still hear Madame Claudine's harsh 'if Lucien fancies you, he'll have you' lurking in the background.

Her eyes rested on the work-bench and she gave a deep sigh. It was a little too late to heed the old lady's advice. She had fallen in love with Lucien and it was more than likely that he would hurt her, but there was nothing that she could do. Except work.

On the day of Madame Claudine's birthday the atmosphere at Bellevigne was one of calm organisation. Flowers were cut from the gardens, jasmine, lilac, honeysuckle and roses, filling the house with their heady perfume. Isabeau, with Jean-Jacques in attendance, dealt with the necessary effects that would determine a successful evening, and the staff, who had been polishing and dusting all week, gave a final flick of their dusters and stood back complacently to view the results.

Troy was anticipating the party with mixed feelings. Lucien was due back during the day, and not even the fact that her work was going well could make her feel anything other than restless and on edge.

She dressed with special care that evening. Lucien had arrived, the Beaufighter rolling silently into the courtyard as she was about to abandon the studio for the day. She had stood by the window and watched him walk from the car into the house, and found that her heart was pounding just seeing that brief glimpse. Somehow she had to find sufficient reserves to meet him calmly. It was not an easy situation to be in. Her presence at Bellevigne was causing talk and speculation, as she had known it would even with all the care she had taken to keep Lucien at arm's length, and to Troy, at least, it was obvious that so far as Isabeau and Madame Claudine were concerned, she was a guest on sufferance.

She found herself giving a sigh and narrowed her eyes critically at the mirror. The Calvin Klein was daring . . . not in its design, which was high-necked and flowing in chiffon, but in the colour, a strawberry red . . . not normally worn by redheads. Troy's hair was piled on to the top of her head, allowing wispy curls to escape above her ears to soften the style, the whole effect emphasising her slender neck and striking features. She purposefully put on a pair of evening shoes with a high heel—if there was nothing else she was going to do that night it was to walk tall!

A liberal helping of her favourite perfume and she was done. Her chin lifted defiantly. The warpaint was on, now for the battle. She would need to call on all her twenty-five years to get her through the next few hours.

As she stepped out from her room and closed the door behind her she could hear the music from the ballroom floating upwards. She walked along the corridor feeling the same nervous chill that she used to suffer before an important job. The chiffon wafted gently against her arms and legs as she moved and the nearer she came to the stairs the less she wanted to go down them.

When a figure turned the corner ahead of her, preparing to descend the stairs, her steps faltered. Lucien saw her, stopped, then walked slowly towards her.

'*Bonsoir*, Victoire.'

'Good evening, Lucien.' Oh, the relief of finding that she had a voice!

'You look magnificent! There will be great gnashing of teeth among the females and admiration in the eyes of all the males!' Lucien took both her hands in his and appraised her with his sardonic grey eyes.

'You look rather magnificent yourself,' returned Troy. She accepted the rising happiness within her at his words just as she accepted the leaping of her senses at the sight of him. Here was the Lucien she had first met, suave and urbane, immaculate in evening suit and pristine white shirt, with flashes of gold at cuff and wrist. His bony, intelligent face was regarding her now with open pleasure, tinged with cynical amusement.

'I think I had better stake a claim for my dance here and now or I'll not stand a chance,' he drawled, raking her with his eyes. 'It's difficult to assess this sophisticated young woman with the dedicated artist in the studio.'

'Which do you prefer?' asked Troy coolly, and Lucien pursed his lips, smiling slightly.

'Oh, I think both have their attractions.' The grey eyes were challenging and Troy said quickly:

'It seems an age since you left for Italy, Lucien, and I've had to wait all this time before I could thank you—about Honoré d'Arcy, I mean. He's such a prominent man in his field and I'm extremely grateful . . .'

'*Sans importance!* I am not interested in your gratitude.'

'But you will surely allow me to thank you,' began Troy, and Lucien broke in briskly:

'I am only interested in whether you like him and if he is able to help you.'

'Lucien, how simple you make it all sound. Of course he is able to help me, he's one of the best men around.'

'*Bon.*' They were now walking towards the stairs. 'I have just delivered the family diamonds to the royal bedchamber. Grand'mère intends to show that even at eighty years, a diamond is still a girl's best friend!' He slanted her an ironical smile.

Troy laughed. They had begun to descend the stairs, Lucien having threaded Troy's hand through his arm, while she placed her other upon the beautifully carved banister. The murmur of guests from the reception hall below suddenly penetrated her senses and she stopped, her eyes flying quickly to Lucien's face, immediately trying to withdraw her hand from his arm. He tightened his hold and calmly continued downwards, so that Troy had no choice but to follow. She was aware of some curious glances from below and was glad when they reached the bottom.

Among general greetings, surrounded by a buzz of noise, Troy found herself being introduced to a tall, rugged fair-haired man, a cousin of Lucien's, who instantly led her on to the dance floor. He spoke excellent English and said with great satisfaction:

'Lucien's duty as host is most convenient, *mademoiselle*! You are enjoying your stay in our country?'

'Thank you, yes,' replied Troy, hoping her colour was fading. 'I'm sorry, I didn't catch your name, *monsieur* . . .'

'Levannier. Raoul Levannier, and since I have already been of service to you, bringing over two suitcases from England, I claim the right to call you Troy.' He grinned, eyes twinkling. 'See, you cannot refuse, and I shall take advantage of your gratitude and book the supper-dance later on.'

Raoul Levannier proved to be Troy's salvation. He was an interesting and amusing companion, claiming cousinship with Lucien on his mother's side and speaking of him with great affection. He kept her informed of the identities of several of the more prominent-looking guests and stayed by her side when she was obliged to say good evening to Madame Claudine, who, he claimed in an awesome whisper, frightened him to death. It was obvious that he was a favourite with his great-aunt, however, and lightened the ordeal considerably.

Troy was not short of partners, although the one man she wanted to dance with did not ask her, and Raoul was always there to claim her at the end of each dance. After a while she began to feel guilty at the way she seemed to be monopolising his time and said diffidently:

'Please don't think you have to stay with me the whole of the evening, Raoul. It's awfully kind of you to look after me . . .'

'Kind?' Raoul drawled the words. 'My dear *mademoiselle*, I'm the most envied man in the whole of the ballroom! If you want to ruin my evening by sending me away . . .' and his face took on a pained look which made Troy laugh, deciding she had done her best.

Wherever she looked she caught glimpses of Lucien as he went about his duties as host. The Descartes had arrived, and Juliette, and were among Madame's select circle of guests. Isabeau was looking very attractive in black and Philippe extraordinarily adult in his evening suit. Jean-Jacques was off duty and danced with Troy, his normally courteous manner melting slightly as the evening progressed.

A light buffet was served during the proceedings, and it was here, in the ante-room where the food and wine was set, that Troy found herself next to Juliette Descartes. Dressed in white and obviously enjoying herself, Juliette prettily confessed that she had asked

Philippe who the stunning girl in red was, and promptly went on to demand to know 'all about' Troy's work in the studio. It was impossible not to like her, Troy thought, for she had such vivaciousness and a happy, friendly personality.

While admitting that she envied Troy her talents she tossed her dark curls and a mischievous gleam came to her attractive green eyes as she confided:

'I am not an academic, but I hope to come out of university with a modest qualification and then plunge into matrimony. Rather old-fashioned of me, isn't it? I wanted to skip university altogether, but my intended husband,' and here she gave a small, appealing moue, mocking herself, 'he wished me to have all the opportunities open to a girl these days, giving me the chance to change my mind.' She laughed happily, piling up her plate with food. 'He is older than I, you understand, and thinks that perhaps I shall become a career-girl or even meet someone nearer my own age. Bah! Me, I know my own mind, but I humour him and my parents. How could I change my mind when I have known and loved him all my life?' She smiled confidently at Troy.

Raoul and Jean-Jacques joined them at that moment and Troy was not obliged to make any reply. She could see Lucien slowly circling the room, stopping to talk to his guests, and her one idea was to escape.

It made no sense, this feeling. Nothing was changed. Juliette's words merely confirmed what Troy already suspected. That there was more commitment on Juliette's side than Lucien's was understandable, girl-hero-worship changing to something stronger and lasting. And on Lucien's side there was the knowledge that the union between the two families would be strengthened.

How ridiculous that the evening should lose its thrill and Troy feel so dead inside, even while she was smiling at the goodnatured banter between Raoul and Juliette and accepting more Charon wine from Jean-Jacques.

Lucien was slowly, but surely, getting nearer and Troy decided she had had enough. She had shown her face and lasted longer than she had intended, due entirely to Raoul's friendly attention, but the time to go was now, before Lucien reached them. She turned to Raoul, who was listening to a lighthearted argument between Juliette and Jean-Jacques, and touched his arm rather urgently. He was immediately courteously attentive.

'Thank you for looking after me, Raoul, but I'll say goodnight and . . .'

'Troy! You're not going?' protested Raoul, surprised and concerned.

'Yes, I'm sorry, I have a headache,' lied Troy, adding quickly: 'It's only just come on. Will you make my apologies to Lucien for me, please? and explain to Juliette and Jean-Jacques. I want to slip away without making a fuss.' She looked at him appealingly and he nodded, a frown on his face, his eyes going round the room.

'Lucien must be somewhere around,' he began, and Troy, who could see Lucien too well, replied urgently:

'I shall probably see him on my way out. No, please, there's no need for you to come,' and giving him a determined smile, Troy wended her way quickly through the crowd of guests.

Even so, it was slow going, and she was stopped by Marcel Dubois and then by Philippe before she finally reached the reception hall. She resisted the temptation to run up the stairs and was halfway up when she heard her name spoken sharply. She pivoted slowly to find Lucien below, one foot on the stair and his hand on the banister.

'You are leaving?' he asked as he began to climb.

'I . . . yes.' Troy swallowed hard, her heart pounding, her eyes caught and held by his.

Lucien came up to her level, his face telling her nothing, and stated: 'We have not had our dance.'

'No, well, you've been busy,' she began awkwardly, and he raised his brows. 'Understandably so,' she added quickly, and he replied:

'And you were going without saying goodnight.'

'I . . . couldn't see you. I asked Raoul to . . . I'm sorry . . . I have a headache,' and Troy turned and left him. She gained the landing and was two steps along before her wrist was taken in a firm grip and she was pulled up short and swung round to him. Lucien searched her face intently, grey eyes bright and piercing.

'Raoul has upset you?'

'No! He has been most kind.' A thought struck her. 'Did you tell him to stay by me?'

He shrugged. 'I suggested that he keep his eye on you. He was happy to oblige. It was no hardship for him.' He quirked a brow. 'You are annoyed? Yet as you are my guest, knowing few people, it was necessary that my mind could be at ease regarding you. If I had known I was to be denied my dance, perhaps I would not have been so sanguine.' Again he lifted his shoulders expressively. 'You wouldn't care to change your mind?' The soft strains of a waltz floated up to them.

'No . . . thank you.'

His eyes narrowed slightly. 'Perhaps another time would be more opportune.' He led her along the corridors until they reached Troy's set of rooms, the music gradually diminishing. Lucien released his grip. For a moment there was a highly charged silence between then, and then his hands went to her hair and he began to take out the combs that secured it in place.

Troy's face was now ashen where before it had been aflame. Every nerve in her body trembled and as her hair tumbled in disarray he cupped her face and kissed her gently. She put out a hand to the door jamb to steady herself. Lucien reached for the handle and pushed open the door. He said softly:

'I hope your . . . headache is soon better, Victoire,' and taking her free hand he raised it to his lips and briefly touched the palm, closing her fingers on the combs.

Troy forced herself to look up, very fleetingly, into his face before turning into her room. She leant back against the closed door, eyes shut in anguish, teeth biting hard on to her bottom lip.

He knew! How humiliating! And damn him for the self-satisfied smile on his face as he walked away! As if he'd proved something!

For the next few days Troy kept as much out of Lucien's way as possible, and in this she was helped by the pressure of his work. He was hardly at Bellevigne, André was either driving him to the airport or else the Beaufighter slid silently out of the courtyard to return some days later a little dustier and André would take pleasure in bringing it back to its original shine.

Madame Claudine invited her more regularly for morning coffee. Troy was wary of these visits, but they passed off without any drama. It was obvious that the old lady considered her no longer a threat.

The only relief from the silly, pathetic pain that twisted like a knife every time Troy saw Lucien was work. A figure of Sable in full flight, tail and mane flying, was coming on well and as an alternative idea, and quite pleasing her, a model of the Bellevigne griffin. She worked longer and harder, driving herself to the limit. She was not sleeping very well and managed to hide her lack of appetite by taking most of her meals at the studio. This, she knew, particularly pleased Isabeau, who was making it plain that she considered Troy to have outstayed her welcome. In this, Troy was inclined to agree with her.

As if to purge herself of Lucien, Troy had begun a likeness of him, working from a batch of photographs that Philippe had taken and which she had kept without him being aware of the fact. When she gazed from the studio window watching Lucien coming or going she would tell herself that she was merely studying the angle of his head, the slant of his brow. She told no one of this piece of work, jealously guarding her secret and keeping the head in a packing case in the corner of the studio when not working on it.

Once Juliette came to stay for a few days, and it was a bitter-sweet irony that Troy liked the younger girl more and more each time they met.

Lucien returned unheralded from a visit to Germany and knocked on the studio door where Troy was working late into the evening. It was lucky that she had had the foresight to lock it, for she was working on his portrait. Hastily placing it in its hidey-hole, she went to open the door.

'Secrets, Victoire?' Lucien asked, as he stepped in, his eyes darting shrewdly round the studio.

Troy closed the door and pushed back a piece of flopping hair with the back of her hand, crossing to the sink to wash the clay from her fingers.

'Hello, Lucien, have you just got back? Had a good trip?'

She glanced over her shoulder and found that his prowling had brought him to the two modelling stands on which Sable and the griffin were displayed. A quick look in the corner showed that the sacking was securely in place and his portrait safe from his inquisitive eyes.

Looking up, Lucien answered: 'Yes, thank you, everything went satisfactorily.'

'Would you like coffee?' Troy asked, uneasily aware that she was now the object of his scrutiny. 'It's nearly ready and I was just about to have a cup.'

'Thank you, that would be pleasant,' agreed Lucien, dropping into the armchair, his eyes still on her. 'Philippe tells me that you have been working very hard. I can see that is true. You have nearly finished them.' He turned his gaze back towards the sculptures, a thoughtful expression on his face. Troy busied herself with the cups, something warning her that this was no innocent, casual visit. Was he about to tell her of his engagement to Juliette? she wondered bleakly. Jean-Jacques had let drop on one of their early morning rides that Juliette was nearing her twenty-first birthday and coming of age. That would be a good occasion, Troy realised, for an engagement party. She set her face into amiable lines and carried the tray over to where Lucien was sitting, replying:

'Sable is more or less finished. Monsieur d'Arcy wishes to see him on my next Thursday visit. The griffin I'm not totally satisfied with, he needs a little more consideration.'

'You have great talent, Victoire.' The words were spoken quietly and Troy's eyes flew to his, startled, the flush of pleasure spreading over her face and receding as quickly as it had come, leaving her starkly pale. She turned back to the coffee things, saying gruffly:

'They're not bad. I . . . I'm quite pleased with the way they're going.'

There was amusement in his voice. 'Quite pleased? Oh, modest Victoire! My sources tell me that d'Arcy is an irascible man, much given to raising his voice in sarcasm to his pupils, but that he is at his most dulcet when dealing with *la belle anglaise.*'

Troy gave a short, embarrassed laugh. 'Nonsense! I don't know who your sources are. I get my share of his bark.' She passed him his cup.

'Talent, however, is no good without stamina,' Lucien remarked mildly, and, a little perplexed, Troy sat back on her heels, staying the pouring of her own coffee, her face questioning. 'You are working too hard and not eating enough. I have left you alone all these weeks because I know how paranoid you artists can become when you're working, but this is ridiculous. I would hazard a guess that you have lost weight since you came to Bellevigne. My dear Victoire, this must cease instantly. I know that your work is important to you, but how can you work if your health goes?'

Troy found that she was trembling, the concern in his voice nearly her undoing. She rose to her feet and began to straighten the tools on her work-bench.

'There's nothing the matter with me, Lucien . . .'

'Even Philippe is concerned! Philippe! Who never notices anything!' She heard him get up and cross the floor to stand behind her. She froze. 'He says that you're not happy, my dear . . . is this so?'

She said brightly: 'Poor Philippe! He doesn't understand the artistic temperament, I'm afraid. Of course I'm happy, Lucien, but you're quite right. When the working mood overtakes me I forget everything else, and perhaps I have been neglecting myself a little lately. It's nothing—really.' She waited, nerves tense, still turned away from him, her hands automatically placing the tools in the correct position for her to find them. She heard him move away and glanced to find him refilling his cup. He said equably:

'So you are going to be a good girl and take things easier, eh?'

Unsuspecting, Troy replied: 'Oh, yes, Lucien—I promise.'

'And you always keep your promises, do you not?'

An oddness in the inflection of his question brought her head round and she looked at him warily, answering: 'I try to.'

'*Bon!* So when I suggest that you spend a few days in Paris as a change from all this hard work,' Lucien went on smoothly, 'you will say—of course I will, Lucien.' He eyed her ironically.

Troy stared, unable to speak.

'My dear girl, I can positively see the excuses whirling round inside your head. A few days in Paris. Come now, the first time we met you admitted that you adored Paris . . . and I find I am suddenly desirous of showing her to you. Won't you pander to my whim, Victoire?'

Troy spoke quietly. 'You have to go on business?'

Lucien waved a dismissive hand. 'There is some business to be attended to,' he agreed, 'but it will not take all of my time. You will be able to keep your Thursday class with Honoré d'Arcy and it will be a good opportunity to visit the lawyers and have advice concerning your inheritance from Bellevigne.' He watched her, sardonic amusement on his lean face as though he knew the battle was won before it had even begun. He sat down and began to glance through one of Philippe's photographic magazines that had been left there.

Troy collected her cup and sat down on the sofa, drinking the coffee and reflecting. A feeling of calm spread over her. The time had come. The moment was right and Lucien, with his instinctive perception, knew it. Her work was finished, bar a few minor details, and when that was done there was no excuse to remain here at Bellevigne. He was right, too, about her health. She was nearly at the end of her tether, emotionally and physically. Lucien's shrewd assessments were no more to be ignored than his bodily presence.

If her time at Bellevigne had shown her nothing else, it was that Lucien held her happiness and her heart-break in the palm of his hands. It was entirely up to her as to whether she was willing to taste the heady delights, knowing there was no future for her with him. *Qui ne risque rien n'a rien* . . . who risks nothing has nothing.

There was no decision to make. She longed now to fall to her knees before him and take those hands and kiss them, bury her face in their palms and feel them move slowly, tenderly over her hair, to rest beneath her chin, lifting her face to his so that he could kiss her lips. So vividly could she know how it would be between them it was almost a surprise to find herself still seated on the sofa. How she stopped herself from making her longings become real she did not know, only that here and now was not the time nor the place. There were too many ghosts at Bellevigne . . . Lucien had already told her that.

She sipped her coffee thoughtfully. There will be no ghosts in Paris. I shall go to Paris with Lucien, she reflected, her whole being tranquil and calm, and he will make love to me. I know it and he knows it, and I shall not say no when the time comes because I need his love and I want him as much as he wants me. We shall behave like civilised people. I shall return to England and Lucien will come to Bellevigne. What happens after that is none of my concern.

The cup was taken from her inert hands and her eyes flew open.

Lucien said gently: 'Come . . . you are nearly asleep.' When they reached the door to her suite, Troy asked:

'When shall we go?'

Lucien said: 'The day after tomorrow.' He raised her hand and brushed his lips across the palm. '*Bonne nuit*, Victoire.'

'Goodnight, Lucien,' whispered Troy.

He gave her a gentle push, helping her on her way, and closed the door behind her.

CHAPTER SEVEN

THE view from the top of the Eiffel Tower was magnificent, even on a day when the sky was not so blue as usual. Troy walked slowly round the observation platform, Lucien indulgently following, savouring this bird's eye prospect of the city as it spread before her, a patchwork of boulevards, greenery and buildings, with the snake-like path of the Seine and its many straddling bridges recalling the eye.

Troy turned her head into the wind, trying to free a strand of hair blown across her face, and found that Lucien was watching her. Hemmed in as they were by the other sightseers, Troy felt a stab of amusement as he waited patiently. She smiled, saying teasingly:

'Poor Lucien, are you dreadfully bored?'

He smoothed back the lock of truant hair. 'No one, *ma chère* Victoire, could possibly be bored with you. I was merely considering that La Tour Eiffel must be the most loved and yet the least lovely of all our monuments in Paris.'

'Oh, hush!' she protested laughingly, touching his lips with the tips of her fingers. 'You'll be lynched by the mob!'

He grinned. 'I agree that it does offer a panorama unparalleled elsewhere.' He turned her to face the view. 'See—the Palais de Chaillot, the Arc de Triomphe,' and he stretched his arm to point out various landmarks.

Troy leaned back against him, happy to listen, content for his cheek to rest against hers as he looked over her shoulder, guiding the direction of her gaze, her body warmed and sheltered by his.

They had been in Paris for four days, four memorable sightseeing days, visiting museums and art galleries, palaces and churches, gardens and parks. They explored the streets of Montparnasse, Montmartre and St Germain, browsing through book and antique shops, watching pavement artists and drinking and eating at pavement cafés and bars.

In the evenings Troy had been introduced to gastronomic delicacies at Lucien's favourite restaurants, the head waiter of each welcoming him in as an old and valued customer, treating 'Monsieur le Comte' with deferential respect and Troy with discreet admiring interest. After such splendid evenings, when gradually their likes and dislikes, theories and philosophies were explored, like a voyage of discovery, Lucien would see Troy safely to her hotel and take his leave. By the time he arrived back at his apartment Troy was ready for bed, waiting for his telephone call.

The first night this happened the reason of his call was to alter the time for their outing the next day, but the second night no excuse was made. Troy would lie and listen to his voice, would smile and softly laugh and talk, content to allow Lucien to shape her future, not understanding the waiting game he was playing but willing to abide by it.

'What would you like to do this evening, Victoire?' Lucien asked, stretching lazily. They had come down from the summit of the Tower and had boarded a river boat and were now having lunch travelling down the Seine. Troy removed her absorbed gaze from the passing scenery and allowed it to rest on her companion. It was no hardship. She smiled happily and rested her chin on palm, elbow on table.

'I don't mind, Lucien. I leave everything to you.' She met his look serenely, the colour deepening slightly in her cheeks as he gathered her free hand in his and murmured:

'Is that so, Victoire?'

The moment was broken by the arrival of food. With wonder and mock apprehension, Troy asked:

'The oysters were delicious, but what, Lucien, I beg of you, is this?'

Straight-faced, Lucien replied: '*Anguille Frite Orly.*' His face broke into laughter at her grimace. 'Truly, it is a delicacy! Trust me, Victoire.'

'I suppose there's a first time for everything,' returned Troy, 'even for tasting fried eel.'

His eyes teased. '*Naturellement*, and I am overwhelmed by your faith,' he added, as her fork went resolutely to her mouth.

Chewing with dainty precision, Troy pronounced: 'Mm . . . distinctive. I believe I shall survive.'

If the trip was supposed to give her memories of a river-boat picture of Paris it was not entirely successful. She was hardly aware of the changing backcloth, was more conscious of the man than the view. Everything faded into the background—the noise, their fellow passengers, the moving scene—the centre of her focus was Lucien. Lucien laughing, the lines in his face deepening, eyes crinkling, resting upon her with teasing tenderness. Lucien, serious, explaining some point of history. Lucien, the host, offering her more wine. Lucien . . .

'I think Les Halles tonight,' mused Lucien. 'A nice crowded, stuffy night-club with a good jazz band, perhaps? Nothing to offend the eye, of course,' he promised, face deadpan.

'Of course,' agreed Troy demurely. She looked up at the sky. 'Lucien, do I see rainclouds gathering?' she asked in amazement. 'I can't believe it!' Sitting under the boat's awning they had been unaware of the changing weather. Lucien gave an exclamation of annoyance and Troy said soothingly: 'Perhaps it will pass.'

As the boat slid into its mooring Lucien took Troy by the hand down the gangplank and they began to run.

Bubbling with laughter, Troy exclaimed: 'Lucien! A little rain won't hurt me—I'm English, well used to it, remember?'

Huge spots began to fall, quickening zealously until by the time they collapsed into a laughing heap in the back of a taxi they were very wet.

Lucien gave instructions to the driver and leaned back, turning with rueful apology to Troy, offering her his clean, folded handkerchief.

'Poor Victoire, this is how I look after you. Here, take this, but I doubt it will do much good.'

Troy, amused, obligingly mopped her face, and then did the same for Lucien. The windscreen wipers were going rapidly, barely able to control the deluge, and Lucien began to give directions to the driver, saying quickly to Troy: 'I have told him to take us to my apartment, it is nearer than your hotel.'

The taxi drew in at the kerb. Lucien delved in his pocket for the fare and thrust open the door, prepared to make a dash for it. Troy, delighting in teasing him, refused to be hurried across the pavement, taking in the beauty of the boulevard and its gracious houses, tall terraced town houses in white stone, now darkening with the lashing rain.

As she stood, face heavenwards, laughing as the rain splashed her face, Lucien gave up and watched her, revelling in her zaniness. He said something she did not hear and gripping her by the shoulders he drew her closer, shouting:

'You're beautiful and quite mad!' and brought his mouth down on hers, hard. They drew apart, laughter gone. Their hair was plastered flat, water trickling down their faces. Lucien took her hand and urged her to run, up the steps, into the lift and along the thickly carpeted corridor, and then into the quiet apartment.

Suddenly it was too quiet. The atmosphere was fraught with tension. Desperately seeking normality, Troy looked around her, curious to discover another side to Lucien, and said in pleased surprise:

'How different from Bellevigne . . . so modern!'

On his way to the bathroom, Lucien observed with dry amusement:

'I have a fairly catholic taste. Do you like it?'

Troy murmured: 'Oh, yes, in its own way it's perfect. Lucien, surely this is a Picasso?' There was awe in her voice, and returning, carrying a large towel, Lucien agreed: 'Yes, an early one, in his Blue Period.'

'And a Bonnard! I like that.' She stood quietly, oblivious of her wet state, her eyes moving on to a couple of Abstracts. He said:

'That is an André Masson . . . and this, a Jean Dubuffet.'

'Oh.' Troy looked doubtfully at the two pictures, a slight frown creasing her forehead. 'I quite like the Masson,' she declared at last, 'I think it could grow on me, but I'm not sure of the Dubuffet.'

'You must let me know. If you can't like it, I shall take it down.'

The words penetrated and Troy swung round, the colour rising in her cheeks.

'Why should you do that, Lucien?' she demanded

gravely, her heartbeat accentuating.

'Because it pleases me to make you happy.'

She savoured the reply which was given in an almost resigned, defensive manner. She said softly: 'Do you, Lucien?' and he burst out:

'You damned well know I do. Victoire, I was determined to keep my hands off you . . .'

Her voice trembled with laughter. 'Were you, Lucien?' His shirt had become almost transparent. She could see tanned skin and the dark hairs on his chest through the wet material. She could feel her own dress sticking to her body like a second skin. She shivered.

Lucien said angrily: '*Mon Dieu*! You are cold . . .' He opened up the towel and enveloped her in it. Troy raised her face to his.

'No, no, Lucien, I don't shiver because I'm cold,' she protested, feeling shy and scared and happy all at the same time. Her voice gained confidence. 'See, my hands are warm,' and she placed her palms inside his shirt, feeling the thump, thump of his heart and the fiery heat from his body.

Lucien gripped her wrists, his voice stern. 'Do you know what you are doing, Victoire?'

The towel slipped to the floor. Troy pressed her forehead against the damp curve of his neck and shoulder and said apologetically:

'Er, no, Lucien, actually . . . I'm hoping you'll teach me.'

There was silence between them for a moment and then Lucien's hand forced her chin up, his eyes bright and intense as he studied her face. Then his own softened and his eyes crinkled. He eased her body to fit in with his and kissed her lids gently, brushing his lips lightly down her cheek to briefly caress her mouth. His breath was warm against her skin.

'First, for the sake of our health, it would be advisable to shed our wet clothes.'

Troy allowed herself the pleasure of thrusting her fingers through his hair and then down his neck and along his shoulders.

'That ... seems a reasonable idea,' she told him breathlessly.

'Actually,' mocked Lucien lovingly.

Troy woke slowly, wondered momentarily where she was, and found Lucien watching her.

'You're beautiful,' he said softly, and she smiled and said dreamily:

'So are you.'

He gave a yelp of laughter and she moved her head more comfortably into the hollow made by his shoulder. She curled her body into him, her arm spread across his chest and she felt his hand come up to touch her hair.

'I shall never forget this day,' she murmured.

'I wonder if I erred a little, placing myself in the position to be remembered side by side with the Eiffel Tower and fried eels?' he ruminated, his voice quivering with amusement. 'Not very romantic, *ma chère*.'

'But rather apt,' replied Troy mischievously. 'Considering I once called you a slimy reptile!' She exploded into helpless laughter as Lucien rolled her over until they were a tangle of sheet and body, unable to move. 'And a bully!' she reproached, helpless. She lay quiet, her face so close to his that she could see the tiny flecks of gold in the grey of his eyes and laughter died as their lips met. They lay silent, conscious of heart and pulse beating in unison.

Lucien said at last: 'How long it seems have I wanted your glorious hair spread upon my pillow and to feel you close to me, like this.' He lifted himself on to one elbow, gazing down on her. Troy found herself colouring beneath his look, a shy confusion sweeping over her. He bent his head and traced her eyes, nose and cheekbone with light kisses and deliberately continued the path down the graceful slope of her shoulder and fullness of breast, lingering tantalisingly for a moment before returning to claim her lips. Then, with the sudden change of mood that Troy was beginning to expect, he gave her bottom a resounding smack and unrolling her free of the sheet, said bracingly:

'Come, my Victoire, we have much to do.' He swung himself from the bed and stretched. 'We have to go to your hotel and fetch your things, contact Jean-Jacques to say we're staying on for a few more days . . .' He looked down at her and laughed. 'If you think that winding a sheet around you is a form of modest decency then I have to tell you that it fails abysmally. In any case,' and here he swept her up into his arms, 'I already know, intimately, how your beautiful body looks.' Trailing the sheet, he stalked through the apartment, elbowing open another door. 'Here is the guest bathroom. I warn you that another pleasure I have been long looking forward to is sharing your bath, but that is for another day.' He stood her down and grinned foxily. 'Twenty minutes is all you get,' and he whipped away the sheet and closed the door.

Troy stared at the girl in the mirror. The image of tousled hair, full and swollen lips and an air of languid satisfaction met her gaze.

Troy Maitland, you are lost, completely lost, she told the mirror, and you don't give a damn!

There followed seven unbelievably happy and enchanting days and nights.

The days were spent riding in the early mornings on

hired horses in the Bois de Boulogne. This could be followed by shopping sprees when Lucien showed a shrewd perception for what suited Troy, overruling her protests that she had had enough spent on her. They lunched at the Café de la Paix and in the evenings joined fellow patrons at l'Opéra or the Comédie-Française, sampled the new experimental theatre at the Espace Pierre Cardin or spent a couple of hours at the Cinémathèque. Days full of companionship and laughter, culture and history, lazy walks and energetic rides.

The nights were spent seeking, searching and learning the shape and the feel of flesh and bone, smoothness of skin and silk of hair, of exploring the capacity to give and take and exchanging words of love whispered in the darkness.

Seven days . . .

On the eighth, Troy had her class with Honoré d'Arcy. Arriving back at the apartment in the late afternoon, she paid off the taxi and found Lucien working at his desk, surrounded by papers. He put down his pen and swivelled round the chair, pulling her on to his lap.

'Mm, you're a welcome diversion to work and a sight for sore eyes,' he observed, returning her kiss in full measure. He settled her more comfortably and smiled lazily. 'How's it gone today?'

Troy rested her head on his shoulder. 'Quite well. D'Arcy has kept Sable. He made the plaster cast today as a class lesson and I can pick it up any time after twenty-four hours.' She linked her hand with his and raised it to her cheek. 'And yours? How has your day been?'

He gave a lopsided smile. 'Not so bad. Missed you. Had to compensate with old Georges Brissac instead, not much of an exchange.'

'Georges!' Troy chuckled, remembering. 'Dear old Georges and the geraniums!' She slanted him a glance. 'Does he know about us? He was awfully keen to get us together, wasn't he?'

'He knows you're Victoria Courtney's granddaughter,' Lucien stated, and seeing her surprise, added: 'Georges is my lawyer.'

'Good gracious.' Troy sat up, digesting this piece of information.

'Brissac and Brissac have been looking after de Sève interests for many years. I told him, by the way, that you'll be coming along to have a chat with him, but you must get a second opinion from another lawyer as well.' Lucien kissed the end of her nose and tipped her off his knee. 'Go and get me a drink, *petite anglaise* . . . a good strong one.'

Troy ruffled his hair and went to oblige. As she mixed the drinks a feeling of despondency crept over her. Reality had reared its ugly head, in the shape of Georges Brissac. How easy it was to grasp happiness in both hands and ignore facing the consequences. How easy to become greedy and forget the promises made to oneself that the end, when it came, would be treated with stoical calmness. Play the game and count the cost. Georges Brissac now reminded her that the time was rapidly approaching when the final reckoning was in touching distance. At least the last seven days had helped her to decide what to do with her inheritance. There was no future for her at Bellevigne, why twist the knife by nurturing the link? Much better to sever everything, even a dry letter from Georges at regular intervals. He would be bound to give her news of Lucien and Bellevigne, and that she could not bear.

Lucien broke into her thoughts. 'By the way, we had a visitor this afternoon—Juliette. She was sorry to have missed you.'

Troy dropped the ice into the glass and watched it settle in the liquid. When Lucien received no reply he looked up from his paper work. Something, probably the stillness, the way she was staring down at the glass, must have registered with him, for he asked: 'What's the matter?' and when she continued to remain silent, added abruptly: 'I thought you liked Juliette?'

Troy turned and said flatly: 'I do.' Her face was pale and she stared at Lucien as if she had never seen him before. 'You told her about us?'

Lucien rose to his feet. 'I told her a little, not all. You mind? I'm sorry . . . I have known her all her life. Juliette is young, but being so, has no old-fashioned prejudices. She can be trusted to hold her tongue and is realistic enough to understand that these things happen. She is happy for us.' He frowned, raising his hands expressively in bewilderment. 'What is the matter, Victoire? Tell me.'

Troy began to shake. 'I don't understand you at all! Is Madeleine happy for us too?'

Lucien's face went blank. 'Madeleine?'

Troy said wildly: 'Yes. Madame de Vesci! Please don't tell me you've forgotten *her*!'

'Of course I haven't forgotten her, but I didn't realise you were acquainted with Madeleine de Vesci.'

Troy knew she should stop. If she wanted to save things between them she should stop, and oh, how much she wanted to. But it was impossible. With a flash of insight she realised that the future had a way of rushing towards one willy-nilly. She could hardly bear to have him look at her with such a cold, forbidding face. Every inch 'Monsieur le Comte.'

She said impatiently: 'I'm not personally acquainted with her, of course, that wouldn't be in the best of good taste, would it? Even in this liberated day and age. Her name, however, has been mentioned in my hearing linked with yours.'

Lucien swung away and began to prowl. He thrust fingers through his hair, saying explosively: '*Mon Dieu*! I do not know how we come to be discussing Madeleine. I had every intention of speaking to you about her, but did not think it necessary as yet.' He swung back, more controlled, voice clipped. 'I have known Madeleine de Vesci for many, many years, first only as a friend, and then later, when she was widowed, as . . .'

'Her lover.'

'Yes, as her lover. The liaison harmed no one. It was not one fraught with possession or passion, rather it was based on companionship and need such as satisfied us both. You hear me say "was." Our association in that way finished a few weeks back, although we remain friends and shall continue to be friends.' He gave an incredulous laugh. 'Good heavens! I do not think that my *chères-amies* have anything at all to do with you, Victoire, so long as they remain firmly in my past. You can hardly have expected that I remained celibate for thirty-four years?'

She declared passionately: 'No, of course I didn't, and your *chères-amies* are nothing to me! Nothing!'

'Then what is this all about.' How did all this start? With Juliette? Juliette has never been, and never will be, anything other than the daughter of a family friend and business associate.' He drew in audible breath and stopped, shot her a look and crossed rapidly to her, pulling her round to face him, searching her face. His lips tightened and his brows came down above half-closed, glittering grey eyes. 'You surely cannot believe that she and I . . .!'

Troy said desperately: 'Not lovers, no ... but Madame Claudine said that it was all arranged. That the marriage settlement was all arranged. She told me, most definitely.'

'And you believed her.' His face was so set and stone-like it could have been her sculpture.

'Juliette herself told me that she was only going through university to please her future husband,' Troy went on feverishly, everything dying away to nothing inside her. No hope now. It was all finished. 'She even s—said that she had known him all her l—life.'

'Jean-Jacques.' The name whipped through the air between them. 'Jean-Jacques Marin. Who has also known Juliette for all her life.'

'Jean-Jacques,' repeated Troy dully.

'*Exactement*! The Descartes, at first, were disappointed when Juliette first informed them, but I have managed to persuade them that Jean-Jacques is an excellent fellow and quite capable of dealing with Juliette, who is no mean handful. He has endeared himself to them by insisting that she goes on with her studies, something they themselves could not bring about, and they are becoming more reconciled. They also realise that when Juliette reaches her majority in a few weeks' time they will either have to consent, or lose her. As for Grand'mère ...' Lucien took a few impatient steps and ended up against his desk, his fists resting on the top, '... she is an old woman who has foolish dreams and fancies.' His head came up and he stared at her with cold, bleak eyes. 'Just what do you think has been happening between us this past week, Victoire?' The words were spaced out meticulously and delivered with scathing intensity.

'I don't know! I thought I did, but now I don't know anything! Why are you so angry? I don't understand!'

'Oh, you don't, eh?'

'No!' She almost shouted the word. 'You've had what you wanted, haven't you? We both have. Almost from the first I've known that this week could happen, and don't you dare deny that you could feel it too, between us, whatever it is,' and she shook her head, her hand to her forehead. 'No, I don't understand.'

'*Évidemment!* To you I cut a very romantic figure. *Mon Dieu!* Engaged to Juliette . . .'

'I didn't think you were engaged—I thought there was an . . . understanding!'

'. . . Madeleine still my mistress—and yet prepared to make love to you! The big seduction scene in Paris. The wining and dining, the presents, the clothes . . . all as a means to an end—to get you in bed with me!'

'You make it sound so simple . . . life's not like that, it's not so . . .'

'All for lust, Victoire!' His fingers gripped her shoulders, his face as white as hers. 'That is how you see me, eh?'

'No, Lucien, not like that—you make it sound so sordid, and it's not been!'

'And you? For what reason did you come to my bed, Victoire? A frivolous holiday affair? Or perhaps . . .'

'Damn you, Lucien! Damn you!' and her hands beat ineffectively on his chest. 'You know that's not true!'

'But I now find that *I* know *nothing*.' He pulled her to him and kissed her fiercely. 'You do not know why I'm so angry? When I meet, at last, the woman who can make me believe in marriage and I find that I am merely an interlude . . . that she considers me to be a Lothario . . . *sacrebleu*! Is that the sort of man you think me, Victoire? Is that the sort of man you want?' He glared at her, nostrils flaring, eyes burning. 'Then that is what I shall be!'

'Lucien, please!'

He covered her words with his mouth, hard and ruthless, ignoring the tears coursing down her cheeks so that they mingled, salty, with the bitter-sweet caress. Troy, too bewildered emotionally, too spent physically, aware that beneath the anger was a great hurt, and loving him too much to resist, lay passive, his own mounting passion, starting as fury, lifting her out of her despair until she was as desperate and as violent as he. Some time during the course of this physical onslaught the tempo changed, the anger became self-orientated, and when they lay, spent and exhausted, there was a curious bond between them, as if this all had been inevitable, from the beginning. Inevitable. And this was now the end.

Lucien stirred after the first few rings of the telephone. He sat up, looked briefly at Troy, ran fingers through his hair and rapidly shrugged on his trousers. Troy stared blankly up at the ceiling, one half of her vaguely hearing Lucien's voice, low and monosyllabic, the words not penetrating, while the other half admired the intricate patterning of the cornice. Lucien came back and said in a curious, flat voice:

'That was Jean-Jacques. Grand'mère has died.' He bent to pick up his shirt. 'André is coming with the car. I should like us to be ready when he arrives.' He began to dress with fierce concentration.

'Of course,' said Troy. 'I'm so sorry, Lucien.' How inadequate words were! She longed to take him into her arms and comfort him, but the sight of his face stopped her. She felt curiously alienated from her body and went through the motions of getting dressed, finding the buttons on her blouse stupidly stubborn.

Lucien was thrusting papers into a briefcase when she came back with her case. Remembering her toilet things, she made for the bathroom. When she reached the door he said: 'Victoire,' and she stopped and waited, her back still turned, and he went on: 'We shall have to talk. Later.' Troy nodded without speaking.

The return journey was taken in almost complete silence. Lucien indicated that André was to continue to drive and sat in his corner, chin resting on fist, staring out of the window. Troy closed her eyes and pretended to sleep, glad of André's presence. He had told Lucien all he knew, which was not much. Madame la Comtesse, he said sombrely, had died of a heart attack and Madame Isabeau was with her at the time.

Once back at Bellevigne Troy escaped to her rooms. She came down for dinner to find only Philippe present. Isabeau had been sedated and Lucien was in his office with Jean-Jacques. From Philippe, who was naturally subdued and upset, Troy learned that his mother had been taking afternoon tea with his grandmother and when summoned by the bell, Zenobie had arrived to find his grandmother collapsed and his mother in hysterics.

After dinner, Philippe went to find Lucien and Troy went back to her rooms. The Château seemed stunned with grief, and she remembered the little old lady's button-bright eyes and her dislike of the English.

She began to pack, and when that was done she made her way over to the studio, skirting the offices as though she was a thief. To her surprise the door was unlocked, the key protruding. The studio looked as though it had been hit by a tornado. Troy walked slowly round, her feet picking their way between scattered tools and broken clay. She halted at the modelling stand and touched a chunk of clay. The griffin was smashed into fragments, and as her shocked gaze went round, seeing the upturned bins and the powdered clay and plaster-of-Paris that had been wildly flung everywhere, she was asking herself blankly: Who would do such a thing? Who hated her enough to do such a thing?

She suddenly flew to the packing case and thrust aside the sacking, sinking to her knees with relief. The portrait of Lucien was intact. It had been overlooked.

How long Troy sat there, hugging the sculpture, she could not, afterwards, determine. She wrapped the head in the sacking and began to pick up and pack away all her tools and equipment. When they were secure in the case she snapped the lock and with some difficulty carried it down to the garage below, which, luckily, was in darkness and deserted. She returned for the sacking bundle, aware of the powdered clay imprint of the soles of her shoes on the wooden treads of the stairs as she left, locking the studio behind her.

Once back in her rooms she sat, fully clothed, in a chair by the window and waited for Bellevigne to settle down for the night. She felt quite calm, curiously so. She realised who had destroyed the studio and could find it in her heart to feel pity. Poor Isabeau! The proud and reserved manner was a façade and inside was a tangle of emotions and frustrations. To have harboured such hate! And what a terrible thing to have to live with, afterwards. That wild loss of control would cost Isabeau dearly. So . . . poor Isabeau.

When everywhere seemed quiet Troy checked the room and placed the envelope, containing the letter she had written earlier for Lucien, on the dressing table. She put the key to the studio next to it.

The M.G. started first go and she blessed it under her breath, waiting a few seconds for the engine to warm up. If her heart gave a sickening lurch at the sight of the beautiful Beaufighter standing alongside, she resolutely gave it no heed. Her eyes turned anxiously towards the Château windows, but no inquisitive light was switched on and the little red sports car crept slowly through the courtyard and out into the drive. Halfway across the park she put on the headlights and sparing no side glance at the two griffins perched high on their stone pillars, she passed through the gateway and out on to the open road, rapidly leaving Château Bellevigne behind her.

CHAPTER EIGHT

'HERE, drink this. I don't want you fainting on my hands.' Fiona handed Troy a cup of tea, hot and strong.

Troy smiled wanly and took an obedient sip. 'I'm not ill, Fiona, just tired.' She lay back in the chair, glad to have reached home, the little breakfast room in their terraced house in Bow giving her a warm feeling of security and commonplace. Almost as if she had never left it, as if the last few months of her life had never happened. Her eyes rested on the two sculptures standing on the table and she felt pain exploding inside her, the first she had allowed herself to feel since leaving Bellevigne. Not much to show for her time away—two sculptures and a broken heart. And a neatly mended scar at the top of her leg.

'What is it about these de Sève men? First your grandmother and now you,' observed Fiona plaintively. 'They have a lot to answer for.'

Troy looked across the hearth and felt the warmth of her friendship with Fiona sweep over her. Dear loyal Fiona! She gave a grimace.

'Be fair, Fiona. I went into this with my eyes open, as no doubt Grandmother did too. She got over it, and so shall I.'

'Of course you will,' agreed Fiona stoutly, yet shot her friend a concerned look. As she drank her own tea she pondered on the fact that Troy had been travelling for nearly twenty-four hours so that the shocked, bruised look in her eyes was hardly surprising.

Troy sat up. 'That was lovely, Fiona. Is there another in the pot?' She handed over the cup, stifling another yawn. 'My body is tired, but I know if I went to bed right now I'd not sleep. My mind is too active at the moment.' She accepted back the refilled cup with a grateful smile. 'Driving through Paris is enough to give you nightmares! I'd have bypassed it if I could have, only I had to pick up Sable from Honoré d'Arcy's studio—thank goodness he was out. I shall have to write and say I've been called back to England unexpectedly. I went from there to Georges Brissac's office. You remember Georges, from the Descartes' party? Luckily he was in. Poor man, he couldn't understand what was happening. He'd been expecting Lucien as well, you see, and when I told him that I wanted to renouce all claim to the de Sève Estate he nearly had a fit. He did everything he could to try and make me change my mind—he's a good lawyer, I'll say that for him. When he could see I was adamant he drafted out a declaration in simple jargon, which I signed, witnessed by a couple of clerks, and then I left him, a worried man. I bet he rang Lucien before the door closed behind me. I headed for the coast and had to wait for a ferry, July is always a busy month, but once on board I did put my head down for a bit.'

'I can never sleep on boats,' Fiona reflected. 'Troy, this signing business. I don't think Lucien is going to like it.'

'Like it?' Troy gave a mirthless laugh. 'He's going to be furious! I've told you how feudal everything is at Sève and Lucien is so used to being puppet-master he'll give Georges hell, but I've signed and there's nothing Lucien can do about it. He can forget all about the Courtneys and the Maitlands!' If he wants to, she added forlornly to herself.

'These are the best you've ever done,' Fiona declared, studying the sculptures closely. 'What does Monsieur le Comte think of his portrait?'

Troy hesitated briefly. 'He doesn't know about it.'

'Oh,' said Fiona blankly, and then: 'At least that awful woman didn't get her hands on it. How could she have done such a terrible thing?'

'She just lost control for a while. She's possessive and jealous and could see her world crumbling and smashed out at what she thought was causing it. I was the catalyst. She would be horrified afterwards at what she'd done.'

'So she should be. I think she was probably a bit in love with Lucien herself,' asserted Fiona, and Troy looked up in surprise but made no comment. Instead, she said slowly:

'Fiona, Georges Brissac told me something, back there in his office when he was trying to persuade me not to sign, something I could hardly take in at the time. He said that there was every indication that Grandmother was in the early stages of pregnancy when she returned to England.' Fiona stared and Troy gave a small shrug. 'I suppose that makes more sense of the regular payments, doesn't it? Valéry de Sève would want to support his child.'

'Your mother,' stated Fiona, and Troy nodded, saying reflectively:

'It also makes sense of why she married so soon. Since hearing the story that bit had niggled me, it seemed out of character, but if a child was on the way . . .' She broke off and frowned. 'My grandfather must have loved her very much, knowing that, and my mother always spoke warmly of him, so he must have treated her as if she'd been his own.'

'Is there any proof?'

'No, not really, only the dates, but it's accepted as a fact by the de Sèves . . . Philippe and then, in turn, Lucien.'

'In which case Lucien is going to be even more furious about the paper you've signed,' pointed out Fiona, and Troy shrugged.

'A slap in the eye for de Sève responsibility, isn't it? He'll just have to realise that I refuse to become one of his dependants. I will not be beholden to him. At least,' she added lamely, 'not by reason of anything that happened years ago.'

'Troy, that makes you Lucien's half-cousin,' stated Fiona thoughtfully, 'and talking of cousins, did you meet Raoul Levannier, the feller who came for your cases? He's become quite a visitor here.'

'Has he? Yes, I met him and thought him rather nice.' Troy eyed her friend speculatively.

'He was telling me about Bellevigne. It sounds impressive.'

Troy's face lightened. 'It is, Fiona, you'd love it.' Bellevigne! Would she ever see it again? And Lucien—would she feel his arms holding her close, hear him whisper her name, tremble at his touch?

Saying goodnight to Fiona, Troy wearily made ready for bed. She closed her eyes and a kaleidoscope of memories taunted her, and she tossed this way and that, seeing Lucien's face, always smiling his tender, teasing smile, until she allowed herself the luxury of tears and, at last, fell into exhausted sleep.

London, for the whole of August, lay under a heat haze. For the third day in succession Troy met Fiona's concerned questioning gaze as she emerged from the bathroom. Pale-faced and feeling wretched, she smiled wanly, saying:

'I'm more like Grandmother than I realised!'

'Are you going to tell Lucien?' asked Fiona, and Troy shook her head.

'No, and you mustn't. Promise, Fiona.'

'Okay, I promise.' She searched Troy's face and went on gently: 'Don't you think he ought to know, Troy?'

Troy swallowed, fighting nausea. 'Yes, but I have some pride left.' She hesitated and added: 'If he comes, then I'll tell him.'

'Ah!' breathed Fiona with satisfaction. 'If he doesn't come for you he'll be a fool, and from all I've heard of Lucien de Sève he's no fool,' but Troy merely shook her head and made no reply.

Later that day she entered the art gallery where the exhibition was being held. She was met at the door by the owner, who was looking extremely pleased. He took her hand and shook it warmly, saying:

'My dear Miss Maitland, excellent news! We've sold the horse and the bust as well, if you'll only change your mind.'

Troy's delighted smile faded. 'Mr Honeycomb, you know the bust isn't for sale,' she said firmly as they walked over to the stand. She saw the small 'sold' disc attached to the card and felt a glow of pride as she looked at Sable. Then her eyes went on to the portrait of Lucien and she said again: 'That's still not for sale.'

Mr Honeycomb spread his hands. 'There's time to change your mind. Personally, I think you have a good chance of being placed among the top few with the bust. There's strength and depth of character in that piece of work.'

Like there is in the original, thought Troy, a sharp stab of pain shooting through her.

Mr Honeycomb glanced round with satisfaction. 'The entries have been most gratifying and the number of sales already encouraging.' He saw Troy smoothing the tips of her fingers along Sable's back. 'The horse looks good, cast in bronze, doesn't he? The same with the bust. Amazing what a difference it makes. Think hard about selling the bust, Miss Maitland. You can't afford to be sentimental in this game, you need sales to earn a living and provide publicity.'

Troy smiled gently. 'I know you're right. But the bust isn't for sale.' Not until I can get Lucien out of my system, not until I can bear to part with it, she told herself. How hard it was, being afflicted with a memory.

Mr Honeycomb proved to be right in his prediction that Troy would be a prizewinner. Standing in a packed gallery, Troy heard the judge call out 'Exhibit twenty-three. Head of a Man in Bronze. Victoria Maitland. Third Prize'. Sable was given a 'highly recommended' and she spent the next hour in a daze, being photographed with the other successful candidates, drinking sherry with the judges and having her hand shaken by strangers.

At a suitable moment Mr Honeycomb drew her to one side and said:

'Miss Maitland, the buyer for Sable is in my office and I was about to go and explain to him that the sculpture must remain in the gallery for another month. Normally clients don't mind—the honour, you know, of purchasing a prize winner. Perhaps you could explain that to him yourself?'

Troy followed him to his office. She had been introduced earlier to the buyer, a bald-headed, shrewd-looking Scotsman, and she supposed the least she could do was to explain, after the man had bought her work.

Mr Honeycomb said: 'I'll see that you won't be disturbed,' and opening the door he ushered her in, closing the door behind her.

The man standing at the window, staring out on to the New Bond Street traffic, turned at her entry.

'*Bonjour*, Victoire,' said Lucien.

Troy felt the colour come and go rapidly in her face. There was no one else in the room. Only Lucien, looking very Lucien-like. Dark charcoal suit, pin-stripe shirt, dark tie, highly polished shoes, and his face, so familiar and yet a little austere at the moment, grey eyes enigmatic.

'Won't you sit down?' Lucien politely gestured to a convenient chair. 'Honeycomb has kindly placed his office at our disposal.'

Of course he has, thought Troy, her heart thumping away like mad. Honeycomb can recognise an influential client when he sees one. He can also recognise Head of a Man in Bronze. His curiosity must be killing him!

Fighting for composure, she said quietly: 'Hello, Lucien. This is a surprise. I was expecting someone else. How are you?' and she sat down, glad to do so, her legs weak and trembling. She forced herself to meet his look and called on all her reserves to hide her feelings. Why had he come? His expression was not particularly a friendly one, but neither was it unfriendly. Impartial . . . and her heart sank. He had come, as of course she had known he would, but merely to tidy the ends, to satisfy his Lord of the Manor upbringing.

'You were expecting Donaldson, my agent over here,' he was explaining, briefly dismissing the bald-headed Scotsman, 'and I'm very well, thank you.' He took his favourite perch, on the edge of Honeycomb's desk. 'And you? But there's no need to ask, I can see for myself—you are as beautiful as ever. And successful. Do allow me to congratulate you on winning third prize.' He folded his arms across his chest and considered her thoughtfully. 'I gather it's not for sale?' He waited for a reply and when one was not forthcoming, went on: 'Of course, now that it has been placed third in the exhibition you can command a much higher price.'

'It is not for sale,' replied Troy with desperate control.

Lucien raised his brows. 'That interests me deeply.' He waited again and when she did not speak, continued smoothly: 'It's fairly reasonable why I want to buy it. I'm flattered that this poor face of mine should inspire anyone to produce such a work—the egotist in me rearing its ugly head. Forgive me! The pun was not intended.' He smiled cynically and after another encouraging pause, added mildly: 'I should have thought you'd be glad to get rid of the thing. After all, it must remind you of an association you would prefer to forget.'

Troy rose to her feet. 'I don't wish to discuss the matter. If you'll excuse me . . .'

Lucien also stood. 'If you insist. But first, I must give you my cheque for Sable.'

Like a zombie Troy sank back into the chair while Lucien took his time seating himself at the desk, bringing out first his cheque book and then his pen. As he wrote he went on conversationally: 'Georges sends his regards, by the way. What an amazing effect you do have on the poor fellow. Each time he sees you he goes to pieces.' He looked up briefly and Troy wanted to get up and run, away from this stranger. Instead she murmured:

'He was most helpful.'

'Too helpful. Thank you for the flowers for Grand'mère's funeral. Most kind and forgiving of you, considering she had made it plain that you were not welcome at Bellevigne. Would it make it any better for you if I tell you that she knew who you were? I did wonder, and found evidence when clearing out her bureau. I came across an old, much worn photograph of Victoria Courtney. There is no mistaking the resemblance to yourself. Hence her antagonism. I hope you'll think a little more kindly of her, knowing this.' He pulled out the cheque and wafted it for the ink to dry. 'Philippe sends his love and wants you to know that he is to start as a weekly boarder at Orléans next month.'

'I'm glad,' said Troy, showing a brief warmth in her carefully controlled manner. Lucien, equally polite, gave a cool nod and observed with wintry detachment:

'Yes. One good thing emerging from the disaster.'

Troy visibly flinched, but he went on:

'Everyone at Bellevigne sends their very best wishes. Isabeau sends inadequate apologies. I offer my own. No words can convey . . .'

'Please! I'd rather you didn't . . .' broke in Troy desperately, 'and I really have to go.'

'Very well.' He came towards her and handed her the cheque. Troy took it, stared miserably at it for a few seconds and then tore it in half. She lifted her head and regarded him gravely.

'I find I cannot accept money from you for Sable.' She took a deep breath before saying simply: 'I should like you to have him as a gift.'

'A gift?' The words were softly spoken.

'Yes. To show that we . . . are still friends.' She forced a slight smile. 'Now you can go back to Bellevigne with a clear conscience.'

A flush stained his cheeks. He said shortly: 'I did not buy Sable as conscience money, Victoire.'

'I know you didn't. You wanted the statue and I

want you to have it, for Bellevigne.'

'You give and yet you will not receive. I suppose I cannot make you change your mind about signing away your inheritance?' He paused and Troy looked away, and he went on mildly: 'No, I didn't think I could. Very well, we shall remain friends,' and he held out his hand.

Troy hesitated and then placed her hand in his. The whole of her being, as if her life-force depended upon it, was concentrated on that contact. She stood still, her heart and pulse racing, the colour slowly rising in her cheeks and she tried to pull away.

'And now,' said Lucien pleasantly, retaining his grip, 'as a friend,' and the word was emphasised, 'perhaps you can explain that extraordinary letter you left me before running away.'

'I didn't run away, Lucien . . .'

His voice changed to sardonic mimicry. ' "Dear Lucien, thank you for allowing me the use of the studio. I think it better if I go. I'm sorry, Victoire." ' He gave a short laugh. 'Sorry? Sorry for what, Victoire?'

Troy tugged at her hand. 'Lucien, if . . .'

'Sorry that you had erupted into my life and turned it upside down? Sorry for leaving behind everything associated with me, every little thing that I had bought you, all left behind in neat tidy piles. Who for, Victoire?' His hands came up to grip her shoulders. 'And was I, too, placed in a neat tidy compartment, to be filed away in your past?'

'Lucien, you're hurting me!'

His jaw clenched and a muscle jumped in his cheek. His hold on her slackened and he took his hands away, slowly, saying with some difficulty:

'I beg your pardon. It seems to be a habit of mine . . . hurting you.'

Their eyes met and then she was in his arms and with a sob, Troy held up her face and their lips met with fierce eagerness.

'*Imbécile!*' The word was a caress, torn from him, his hands holding her completely his prisoner. 'How could you believe that for one instant I'd let you go?' He searched her face and kissed away the tears. 'You knew I'd come for you?'

Troy nodded, smiling through her tears.

'Of course you did! You know the de Sève motto—he can hold his own . . . and that is what I am doing. You are mine, Victoire.'

'Yes, Lucien, yes.'

'Did you think I could forget you? *Mon Dieu!* Dealing with Isabeau's hysteria, Philippe stricken and scared, the whole Estate and village in mourning, the funeral and Grand'mère gone—I thought of you constantly, feeding my guilt . . .'

'Hush, there's to be no talk of guilt.' She touched his face, relearning the hollows and bones, his hand coming up to hold her palm against his mouth, to kiss it and tightly clasp it.

'Generous, Victoire, with the memory of that wrecked studio still before me, and you say there is to be no guilt! Can you imagine with what I had to contend? I was raging inside against all my commitments, my duty, everything that kept me away from you. Do you think I did not know exactly how you were and what you were doing?'

Troy gave a gurgle of laughter. 'Monsieur le Comte has only to lift the telephone.'

Lucien smiled grimly. 'You are pleased to think me arrogant and powerful, Victoire, but it is not so. Where you are concerned I have no armour.' His speech ended abruptly as his mouth hungrily found hers, his embrace tightening ruthlessly. It relaxed only enough for Troy to gain her breath and gaze wonderingly into Lucien's eyes as he mocked her gently: 'Well, *mademoiselle*? Are you sorry for running away?'

Troy gave a shaky laugh and hid her face in his shoulder, murmuring: 'Yes, Lucien. I won't do it again.'

'I should think not! Here.' He handed her his handkerchief. 'This is, I believe, where we came in, although it was wine and not tears that was needed to be mopped up. Let us get out of here, my sweet, before we shock Mr Honeycomb too much.'

'More likely to give him grey hairs through curiosity,' joked Troy, and Lucien grinned wickedly, saying under his breath as they left the office: 'We shall find somewhere comfortable and quiet where you can tell me exactly why my poor, ugly face is not for sale.'

Some hours later Lucien remembered that remark and slyly reminded her of it.

'You know why,' Troy murmured. 'I couldn't bear to part with it.' She put her hand in his and let him pull her down into the comforting curve of his arm as he sat on the sofa in the sitting room of his hotel suite. She rested her head on his shoulder. 'I desperately hoped you'd come over for the exhibition, and if you did, what you would think to your portrait . . .'

'My dear girl, I could hardly believe my eyes, and when I found it was not for sale I began to think I stood a chance.'

'Foolish man,' scolded Troy lovingly. 'I was yours, right from the start. When Sable was sold I thought you'd come and the despair I felt when I met your Scotsman because he wasn't you! I then began to think

I'd angered you so much, that day when Juliette came . . .'

'Foolish girl,' mimicked Lucien, lifting her face to his. 'So you thought I wanted you for my mistress, eh? What a blow that was to my self-esteem, and how brutal I was to you! When you left Bellevigne that was all I could think of—that you had gone with memories of anger and not of tenderness and love.' His hand stroked her hair and he went on pensively: 'Of course, until you told me I did now know what Grand'mère had told you. I thought you knew that our future would be together. How could it be otherwise? That very day I saw Georges and told him of my intentions. That, my sweet, is why poor Georges was so bewildered when you came to him the following day intent on washing your hands of us all. That is also why Isabeau destroyed the studio.'

'Lucien, there's no need . . .'

'Yes, there is, my dear.' He fell silent and then went on: 'After the ball I told Grand'mère of my feelings toward you. She was not surprised, and I also told her about Jean-Jacques and Juliette. That day in Georges' office I telephoned Grand'mère and asked her to break the news to Isabeau, so that by the time we arrived home she would have become used to the idea. I have no need to go over Isabeau's neurosis, we both know how possessive and jealous she is where Philippe, the family and myself are concerned. What I did not realise, or perhaps did not want to realise, was how deep these feelings went. How could I conceive that she would go straight to the studio and . . . well, we know what she did. From what I can piece together, when she finally came to her senses she flew straight to Grand'mère and confessed what she had done. Grand'mère succeeded in calming her down and rang for tea. Zenobie says that when she took this in to them they were both sitting quietly discussing the colours of the embroidery Isabeau was working on. Grand'mère asked Zenobie to send Jean-Jacques to her later. However, after Zenobie left and before Jean-Jacques arrived she became ill and had a severe heart attack, which sent Isabeau into further hysterics.'

Troy gave a sigh. 'How is Isabeau now?' and Lucien shrugged.

'Less hysterical, still consumed with guilt, of course. She is with friends in Provence and is having medical attention. Philippe, I need hardly tell you, knows nothing of what his mother did. Only Jean-Jacques and myself know, and we cleared the studio together.'

Troy threaded her fingers through his and said broodingly:

'The minute you told me about Jean-Jacques and Juliette I could see it all clearly. You helped them to be together, didn't you? The ballet tickets, and Jean-Jacques taking papers to Paris to be signed. You brought them together whenever possible.'

'What a ninny you were,' Lucien observed tenderly, 'to think I could marry Juliette.' He gave a short laugh. 'When it became known that I was coming to England the whole of Bellevigne seemed to let out a long-held breath. No one said anything, of course, but Jean-Jacques ordered more clay, Zenobie began to be interested in menus again and André polished the Beaufighter until you could see your face in it. They all made it very clear that you should never have gone in the first place.'

Troy laughed softly, absurdly touched by their approval. 'I didn't want to leave, Lucien, but I'd caused so much trouble. Indirectly, I even caused your grandmother's death . . .'

He shook her roughly. 'Don't talk such arrant nonsense! You might as well say that it was our grandparents' fault, for meeting and falling in love, or mine for telling Grand'mère of our impending marriage. Rather prematurely, as it turned out,' he added wryly.

Troy stirred uneasily, listening to the sounds of the traffic outside Lucien's hotel window. She said a little wistfully:

'I wish Madame could have liked me.'

Lucien sat up and turned her face to his. 'But, my dear, she did, believe me—against her will, almost. She was a proud woman, Victoire, but not an insensible one. Consider. It could not have been easy for her, loving Valéry as she did, to know that she was not his first love. That, but for a quirk of fate, another woman would have married him and borne his children. You were not her first choice as a suitable partner for me, how could you be? You were the granddaughter of her rival, the natural granddaughter of her husband. She was almost bound to be antagonistic toward you. But once I had convinced her that you were the only woman I could ever marry she decided to get to know you better . . .'

'That was after her birthday,' broke in Troy, surprised. 'And I thought she was being kinder because she was confident she would get her own way with you and Juliette.'

'I have proof that she was reconciled to our marriage,' stated Lucien firmly. 'She left instructions that certain items of personal jewelry should go to you.'

Troy turned a glowing face to him, smiling tremulously. 'Oh, Lucien, you don't know how relieved I am to hear you say that! How generous of her.' She hesitated and went on pensively: 'Don't you think it strange how the circle has come round fully?' She chuckled at the look of sceptical amusement on his face. 'No, really, Lucien, almost as if we were meant to come together.'

Lucien's eyes twinkled. 'Helped by our ghosts, perhaps? What do you think to the idea that we are related? Do you like sharing Valéry?'

'You seem so sure.'

'My father was certain, and he was not given to romancing, and the time element is pretty conclusive. However, I am not content with a mere half-cousinship, and intend making our relationship a much closer one.'

Troy gave a slow smile and murmured teasingly: 'I don't think it possible to get much closer than we did, less than an hour ago.'

Lucien considered her with lazy amusement, those quirky eyebrows rising comically. 'My dear *mademoiselle*! spare my blushes and behave.' He settled her back in his arms and gave her a short, hard kiss. 'I am not returning to France without you, so it will have to be by special licence. Will you be disappointed?'

Troy shook her head and mumbled: 'The trimmings don't matter.'

'A woman in a million! and one who realises that anything could be happening to my crop of grapes in my absence. So, I suggest we have a quiet ceremony here, in London, and have our wedding party at the end of the vintage and invite the whole of the district to come and celebrate both events with us.' He lifted a brow. 'Or am I steamrollering you again?'

'Whatever Monsieur le Comte wishes,' said Troy demurely, and was thoroughly kissed for her impudence. Rosy-cheeked and breathless, she added tremulously: 'You know I adore your steamrollering, Lucien. The only thing is, won't all your friends and relations be cross to miss your wedding? After having waited so long for it to happen?'

He gave a bark of laughter. 'Exactly why I want to keep them all away! No, Victoire, do not worry. I shall invite a few special guests who will think nothing of crossing the Channel for so auspicious an occasion. Juliette and Jean-Jacques and Philippe, of course, Raoul . . .'

'Did you know he has his eye on Fiona?' asked Troy.

'. . . probably the Descartes . . .'

'Most definitely the Descartes! Their balcony is a special place,' and they exchanged smiles.

'And you, Victoire, who will you ask?'

Troy considered the question. 'Fiona's parents have been very good to me over the years and I think Mr McKay would walk down the aisle with me.' She slanted him a glance. 'I am allowed an aisle? Not St Paul's, of course,' she added, with a grin, 'but my own church of St Anne's.'

'I think we can manage an aisle,' agreed Lucien. 'And will Mr Hal Lindsey be invited?'

Troy's eyes widened. 'Why, yes, I suppose so. I owe a lot to Hal.'

'Hm.' growled Lucien. 'Invite him, then.' They shared another smile and biting her bottom lip Troy dropped her eyes to her hands and began:

'Actually, Lucien . . .' She stopped as her courage failed her and went on brightly: 'Can we eat? I'm hungry.'

'Then we shall order dinner,' he said, eyeing her thoughtfully. 'Shall we go down to the dining room, or have something sent up here?'

'Here, please,' replied Troy, and while Lucien telephoned their order she went to the bathroom. It had been a long day, and so much had happened, and it was not over yet. She stared at herself in the mirror and thought despairingly: Why it is so difficult to tell him? You know he loves you.

On her return a table had been set with a candelabrum and three candles flickering in the centre. A heated trolley wheeled in by one waiter and another carried an opened bottle of wine which Lucien had just inspected and nodded his approval, which was placed on the table. A bucket of ice sported an unopened bottle of champagne. After assuring the waiter that they would serve themselves, Lucien greeted Troy with a smile and held out her chair.

'Aylesbury duckling and a good red Bordeaux, in England often called a claret,' he informed her, pouring the rich red wine into their glasses. 'As you will be the wife of a *vigneron* your taste-buds must be educated.' He held his glass up to the light, then took a sip. 'Mmm . . . excellent. Good claret is a taste that is not always easy to acquire but is impossible to lose, and this particular wine from the Médoc has travelled well.'

As their meal progressed with fresh strawberries and cream and an assortment of cheeses, Lucien opening the champagne, Troy was tempted several times to drop her bombshell, but the words stuck in her throat. Lucien said at last:

'Your appetite seems to have disappeared, Victoire.'

Troy gave an apologetic smile and allowed herself to be guided to the sofa, Lucien bringing their glasses, and when they were settled he turned to her, taking her hands in his own warm clasp, and saying gently:

'My dear, you had much better tell me what it is

that is bothering you. I'm sure, between us, we can deal with any problems that arise. Won't you trust me, Victoire, to help you?'

Troy's eyes filled with ridiculous tears and she gave a choking laugh. 'Are you always going to know when something is bothering me, Lucien?'

'I hope so.'

She pulled her hands free and said quickly: 'I think I can tell you better if you're not touching me. My wits seem to desert me, and I need them.' She nervously smoothed the material of her dress over her knees and gave him an uncertain look. His calm, patient expression reassured her slightly and she went on more easily: 'Lucien, I know you were furious with me, hurt too, when I thought we were having . . . only a brief *affaire de coeur*, but where you were concerned I never had any confidence in myself. I've always mistrusted my looks, they've never been much help in anything but work—photographic work, I mean—only you did know the other side of me, the side that's important to me, and I found that I wanted to be beautiful for you . . .'

Abruptly, Lucien rose and swung round to face her. 'Victoire, my darling girl, don't you realise that it is the whole you that I love? This includes your wonderful talent—which makes me so proud of you—and your warmth, your humour, your compassion, everything about you is very, very dear to me.'

'Well, I'm beginning to realise it,' she admitted shyly, 'and when I left Bellevigne I never doubted that you would come for me. At least, deep down I didn't, although sometimes in my darkest moments I began to think I'd dreamed what you said—you know, that I was the woman who could make you believe in marriage. But that wasn't often. Mostly I remembered the good things, and then I knew you'd come.' She paused and raised her eyes, regarding him appealingly. 'Do you believe that, Lucien?'

Face slightly puzzled, Lucien replied: 'Yes, Victoire.'

Troy found that she was holding her breath. She gave a small sigh, followed by the makings of a smile.

'You once told me that we ought to feel an affinity with our ghosts, that we look like them and bear their name. The link is stronger than you think, and although there was no future together for them I know there is one for us.' The smile grew a little, cautiously. 'Lucien, despite my good intentions not to follow completely in my grandmother's footsteps, I'm carrying your child.'

There was silence while shy brown eyes locked with blazingly intense, suddenly tender, grey ones. In two strides Lucien gathered her up into his arms and Troy lifted her glowing face to his.

'Maman . . . *qu'est-ce que c'est?*'

Troy peered over the little boy's shoulder at the open book on his lap and replied:

'*C'est un éléphant*, Valéry.' Her finger went to the page. 'See, here is the word written below the picture . . . and I thought we were going to speak English today, *mon petit*, to surprise Auntie Fiona and Uncle Raoul?'

Valéry nodded his dark head, frowning intently over his book.

'*Oui, Maman. Où est* . . . where is the baby elephant, Maman?'

Troy smiled fondly and ruffled his curly mop. 'It's on the next page, as you well know!' and mischievous grey eyes peeped brightly up at her. The study door opened and peering round his mother's knees Valéry gave a whoop of excitement and struggling to his feet, rushed across the room, shouting: 'Papa! Papa! *Il neige,* Papa!'

Lucien laughed and swung the little boy high into the air. The dogs, César and Satan, circled round his legs boisterously. 'Yes, it is certainly snowing, Valéry, and tomorrow we shall build a snowman, eh?'

'Yes, please, Papa.'

Lucien gave his son a hug and set him on his feet.

'Papa, can Aimée help us build a snowman?' asked Valéry, and Lucien knelt, bringing his face level with Valéry's.

'Do you think she could help us, Val?' he asked, and Valéry screwed up his face and shook his head.

'But she will miss all the fun,' he exclaimed, his lip beginning to tremble, and Lucien said quickly:

'Not at all! Maman will hold her up at the window and she will have fun watching us.' This seemed to satisfy Aimée's brother, for he nodded happily and ran to the window, watching the falling snow, his sturdy body flanked on either side by the two dogs. Lucien regarded him for a moment, smiling, and then turned to his wife. Troy, who was knitting a white, delicate garment, sitting in an armchair by the fire, gave him an askance, upward look.

'You've relegated me with Aimée, I see, when you know I'd much rather be helping you menfolk with the snowman.'

'You'll do as you're told until Marcel gives you the all clear.' He bent to kiss her, touching her cheek gently with his hand as he straightened.

'You and Marcel Dubois are a couple of old fusspots. So I am a little run-down after Aimée's birth. Nothing to worry about.'

'And we are not worrying,' commented Lucien, 'merely making sure you behave yourself.'

'Steamrollering me, you mean,' grumbled Troy goodnaturedly, putting down the knitting. 'Will the snow mess up our plans?'

'The roads are still passable, love,' Lucien assured her. 'Philippe telephoned to say he would be a little late, André has already gone to meet the train.'

'And Fiona and Raoul?'

'Raoul is an extremely competent driver, my dear, and they should be here within the hour.'

Troy smiled and relaxed, clasping his hand and holding it against her cheek.

'Is the forecast bad?' she asked.

'Bad enough for Valéry to get his snowman tomorrow. We're in for a hard winter, it seems. However, the snow need not concern us too much at the moment. Food provisions are in, the Christmas tree is decorated,' he glanced at Valéry, 'and a certain little boy's empty stocking is already hanging on his bed, ready to be filled by Santa Claus.' His eyes returned to Troy, twinkling. 'He does well having a foot in each of our countries, does he not? St Nicholas on the sixth of December and Santa Claus tomorrow on the twenty-fifth.'

'As they both come to you too,' returned Troy equably, 'I shouldn't say much.' She paused. 'Philippe did not mention Isabeau?'

Lucien grasped her hand tighter and said gently: 'No. Are you still worrying that she refuses to come?'

'Her visits are so few and far between, Lucien, even after five years.' Troy gave a small sigh. 'I can't admit that she's an easy guest, and that makes me feel even guiltier. After all, Bellevigne is her home.'

'And Isabeau chooses to live away. We have done

our best and can do no more. She is happier down in Provence and Philippe sees her regularly. I will not have you worried over Isabeau, Victoire.'

Troy grimaced a smile and said lightly: 'Very well, Monsieur le Comte.'

The door opened and Gabrielle came in carrying a tray. She smiled a greeting, murmured: '*Monsieur, madame*,' and placed it down on a low table.

'Thank you, Gabrielle,' said Lucien, and the young girl looked across at Valéry, still engrossed in the falling snow, and then turned to Troy.

'It is the little one's supper time, *madame*.'

'Very well, Gabrielle. I shall be up in half an hour, and will you ask Zenobie if cook can hold back dinner by an extra hour, if that is possible?' Gabrielle murmured '*oui, madame*,' and crossed to take Valéry by the hand, whispering something in his ear. Valéry asked anxiously:

'You will come, Papa, to see my boat sail in the bath?'

'I shall,' promised Lucien, placing the palm of his hand gently on the top of his son's head as he passed. 'See that Madame does not tire herself, Gabrielle. The new nanny is competent?'

'*Oui*, Monsieur Lucien, she seems a good girl,' and giving Troy a knowing smile, Gabrielle led Valéry from the room.

'Madame will not tire herself supervising her son's bath,' observed Troy mildly, 'and as for the new girl, she's somewhat shy at the moment and knows no French, but Valéry has taken to her. She comes from a little village in Dorset, so is used to country life.' She watched as Lucien opened the bottle on the tray and began to pour the sparkling liquid into two glasses, and said in surprise: 'Champagne, Lucien? Are we celebrating?'

He handed her a glass. 'We are.' He sat down on the rug in the same spot his son had vacated some time before and Troy ran her fingers through his dark hair and thought how alike they were, father and son. 'You really are feeling better, Victoire?' Lucien now asked, his grey eyes appraising her intently.

'Much better,' she told him firmly. 'Please don't worry about me, darling, I come from some good sturdy stock.'

'Of course I worry,' Lucien said roughly, holding her to him, and Troy replied quickly:

'Yes, I know you do. What I mean is, I have no intention of being a worry to you. Now, what shall our toast be, and what are we celebrating?' She tilted her head questioningly. 'I'm always ready to drink champagne, *mon cher*, but have I been awful and forgotten some important anniversary?'

Lucien shook his head. 'No, no . . . it's just that I had been over to the stables and was walking back to the house, hurrying slightly because I did not wish to miss Valéry's bedtime. For no particular reason I began to think of the other Valéry, Grandpère, and your Victoria, and how they had brought us together, and I was consumed with such a rush of happiness, of well-being, that I wanted to share my feelings with you. I wanted to say thank you from the depths of my heart, for being the mother of my children, for being my wife, and to tell you how much I love you.' The hand on his hair had ceased to move while he had been talking and Lucien swivelled round. He saw the bright, large tears trembling on her lashes and said with tender amusement: 'My dear girl, the last thing I wanted to do was to make you cry!' He stood and gathered her up into his arms, wiping her tears with his handkerchief.

Troy gave a shaky laugh and blew her nose. 'Yes, well, you shouldn't say such beautiful things to me and not expect the waterworks.' They stood holding each other, silent, comfort and love flowing between them. Finally, Troy murmured: 'We must have a toast.'

Lucien suggested thoughtfully: 'Shall we drink to our ghosts for bringing us together? Or shall it be to us, and Valéry and Aimée?'

'Yes, to both,' replied Troy, smiling, and raised her glass. Lucien caught her free hand and raised it to his lips and Troy came to him and their lips met. With his arm round her shoulders Lucien drew her to the window, César and Satan making way for them, and together they looked out at the bleak white landscape of the park, looking eerie in the darkening twilight.

Troy turned her head slightly and found that the room was reflected on the window-pane. She remembered the first time she saw it, when Lucien told her the story of their respective grandparents. It was still her favourite room and she had chosen it to be the most fitting place for Lucien's portrait and her eyes rested on it now, allowing herself a small glow of satisfaction. It really was one of the best things she had done, she thought. The statue of Sable was in Lucien's office and there was a rapidly growing following for 'Troy' sculpture, both in England and France, that was most gratifying.

Lucien shook her gently. '*Hé!* Come back, from wherever you are!'

She looked up and smiled. 'I'd not gone anywhere. I was right here.' Her eyes went round the room reflectively. 'In the final analysis we're not very important, are we? We come and go, but Bellevigne stays.'

'I do believe you're more feudal than any of us,' teased Lucien, and Troy grinned, raising her glass and saying firmly:

'To a house called Bellevigne.' She drank, eyeing Lucien over the rim. He followed suit, and remarked mildly:

'However unimportant you may think us, there are two upstairs who would disagree.'

Troy laughed and tucked her arm companionably through his as they left the study.

'Aimée will be extremely demanding in about twenty minutes,' she agreed, and Lucien added: 'And there is a new boat to launch in the bath, remember?'

They exchanged smiles and together began to climb the stairs.

Harlequin® Plus

PABLO PICASSO

When Lucien showed Troy the Picasso painting in his Paris apartment, he was showing her the work of probably the greatest artist of the twentieth century. Pablo Picasso was born in Spain in 1881 and died in France in 1973 at the age of 92; and on his ninetieth birthday, to celebrate his contribution to art, the city of Paris hung his paintings in the Louvre.

Picasso began to draw when he was very young; his father, an art teacher, gave him his first lessons. As a teenager he attended art school in Madrid and Barcelona. He disliked classes, preferring instead the life of the artists' cafés of Barcelona. In 1900, when he was nineteen Picasso made his first trip to Paris, and for the next four years he divided his time between the two cities. In Paris he was fascinated by the bohemian street life of Montmartre, the artists' quarter. Although he was so poor he was usually on the verge of starvation, he somehow always had enough money to buy a few tubes of paint, with which he portrayed the people of his neighborhood.

It is this stage of his art, during his early days in Paris, that has come to be known as Picasso's Blue Period–named because of the many shades of blue that dominated his paintings. Some art critics believe that Picasso's blues are the blues of misery and despair. The tall, thin, sad-looking people who inhabit the canvases seem to express the artist's own poverty and perhaps also the loneliness he felt away from his native land. Picasso himself said only that, "Blue is so gracious."

But the Blue Period was not to last. In 1904 Picasso fell in love with a woman named Fernande Olivier, and they subsequently spent several years together. It was shortly after they met that blue was replaced in his paintings by dusty pinks and shades of light red. Perhaps his use of these more cheerful colors is a testimony to the influence of love on the work of a great artist.